It was every m

Soft red light gave the room a glow of sinful pleasure. Exotic perfume fragranced the air and a stereo played soft, yet subtly persuasive music with an underlying beat that mimicked the rhythm of lovemaking. Gilt-framed mirrors reflected the centerpiece of the room—a bed covered in virginal white satin.

Reclining on the bed was a woman Mac barely recognized. Although the scraps of white satin covering her breasts seemed inconsequential, they managed to emphasize her cleavage. His gaze traveled to the white lace garter belt and panties, which defined her femaleness in ways he'd never imagined. The garters were fastened to white silk stockings, and on her feet... Mac couldn't quite believe that Tess, a woman who believed in no-nonsense running shoes, was wearing four-inch heels.

Tess gave him a slow smile. "What do you think?"

"I don't—" Mac swallowed. "I don't believe this is about thinking."

"True." Her gaze swept over him. "I have the reaction I wanted. Would you like to get out of those clothes? You seem a bit...overdressed."

He groaned softly and shook his head to clear it. He'd need every ounce of his control to make this the slow seduction he'd planned.

"C'mon, Mac, undress for me," Tess said with a saucy grin. "I'll make it worth your while, cowboy."

Dear Reader,

Not long ago, my sister gave me a gift certificate for an astrological reading. During my hour-long session, the woman informed me that the stars' alignment on my birthday meant a) I enjoy kicking over the traces, and b) I have a very erotic personality! She might as well have told me point-blank to write a Blaze and fulfill my destiny. Which I have proceeded to do.

And did I have fun! When the story called for Tess Blakely to buy books on sexual technique to prepare her for losing her virginal status, what else could I do but throw a few how-to manuals into my own shopping cart? A conscientious writer must research her subject, after all. I had no idea that the sensuality section of my local bookstore was so huge.

My poor hero, Mac MacDougal, is a bit intimidated by Tess's spicy library, but he soon gets into the spirit of discovery. Boy, does he ever. The result is a story that is hotter than an Arizona chili pepper. I claim no particular credit for that. Blame it all on the stars!

Warmly,

Vicki Lewis Thompson

Vicki Lewis Thompson
PURE TEMPTATION

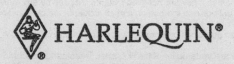

HARLEQUIN®

TORONTO • NEW YORK • LONDON
AMSTERDAM • PARIS • SYDNEY • HAMBURG
STOCKHOLM • ATHENS • TOKYO • MILAN • MADRID
PRAGUE • WARSAW • BUDAPEST • AUCKLAND

To Alex Comfort, M.B., D.Sc.
for celebrating the beauty of love and play.

ISBN 0-373-25844-5

PURE TEMPTATION

Copyright © 1999 by Vicki Lewis Thompson.

Visit us at www.romance.net

Printed in U.S.A.

1

Summer Project: Lose Virginity.

TESS BLAKELY rocked gently on her porch swing, a yellow legal pad balanced on her knee, a glass of iced tea on the wicker table beside her. She gazed at what she'd written and sighed. The beginning of a quest was the hardest part.

It was pitiful that a twenty-six-year-old, reasonably attractive woman found herself saddled with the handicap of virginity, but there it was, on paper. And her status had to change before she left for New York at the end of the summer, or she'd risk her credibility with the high school girls she'd been hired to counsel. Besides, she wanted to experience sex. She *longed* to experience sex.

She took a sip of iced tea and continued.

Goal One: Find knowledgeable candidate willing to deflower me.
Goal Two: Swear candidate to absolute secrecy.
Goal Three: Get it on.

Tess sighed again. Writing out her goals and objectives had been her cherished method for getting what she wanted, beginning at the age of eight when she'd yearned for her very own pony. But although she wanted to lose her innocence much more than she'd wanted that pony, her current project seemed about as likely of success as a personal rocket trip to the moon.

The little town of Copperville, Arizona, wasn't exactly crawling with "knowledgeable candidates," but even the few that she'd consider had been scared off long ago by her four very large, very overprotective older brothers. And not a one of those beefy brothers had moved away or relaxed his vigilance. They all expected their little sis to save herself for her wedding night. They were stuck in the Dark Ages, as far as she was concerned, but she loved them too much to openly defy them.

That was the reason for goal number two—for absolute secrecy. Now *there* was a definite sticking point. Even if she found a man her brothers hadn't intimidated, how could she ever expect him to keep a secret in Copperville? This was a town where you could wake up with a sore throat in the morning and have three kinds of chicken soup at your doorstep by noon.

Which meant she might never arrive at the third step—Getting It On. And she was ready for number three. Extremely ready. She'd driven all the way to Phoenix to buy research books, knowing that she couldn't be caught thumbing through *One Hundred Ways to Drive Him Wild* in the Copperville Book Barn, if the local bookstore even carried such a thing, which she sincerely doubted.

So much for her list. The goals were unreachable. She tossed the legal pad on top of the stack of books lying next to her on the swing. A list might have worked for the pony, but it was probably dumb to think it could cure a resistant case of chastity.

And to be honest, a list might have helped get her

that pony all those years ago, but her best friend, Jeremiah "Mac" MacDougal, had been the real key. Her family lived in town and had no room for a horse, but Mac had talked his folks into keeping Chewbacca on their ranch. Tess's older brothers had always thought they had first claim to Mac, being boys, but Tess knew better. Ever since Mac, who'd been only five at the time, had saved her from a rattlesnake, she'd known he was the best friend she'd ever have.

Mac. Mac could help her find the right guy! She mentally slapped her forehead and wondered why she hadn't thought of him before. Unlike her brothers, Mac understood why she needed to take the job in New York and prove herself an independent, capable woman. Her brothers might have laughed at her when she asked for a light saber for Christmas, but Mac had saved his allowance and bought her one.

Surely Mac would also understand that she couldn't go to New York a virgin. Coming from a small town was enough of a handicap. If the girls she'd be counseling figured out that she was sexually inexperienced, she'd be a real joke. Mac would see that right away. And he'd help her find the right man to solve her problem.

THE SUN HAD BARELY crested the mountains as Mac saddled two horses. He'd left his bed this morning with a sense of anticipation. He hadn't had an early-morning ride with Tess in months. When she'd called to suggest it, he'd been happy at the prospect, although lately he'd been feeling a little jealous of her.

As kids they'd spent hours talking about the places they'd go when they were older. This September she was actually going to do it, while he was stuck on the ranch. His folks expected him to stay around and gradually take over what they'd worked so hard to build. As the only child, he couldn't foist off that obligation on anybody else.

Tess had it easier, although she was forever complaining about how hard it was for a woman to "go on a quest," as she put it. But she was doing it, and he wasn't. Her mom and dad hated having her leave town, especially for some faraway place like New York City, but they still had four sons, their wives and seven grandchildren. With such a slew of Blakelys around, Tess didn't have to feel guilty about grabbing her chance at independence. Mac envied her that freedom.

"Top 'o the mornin' to ye, MacDougal."

He buckled the cinch on Peppermint Patty and turned to smile at Tess. She used to greet him that way for months after she'd starred in Copperville High's version of *Brigadoon*, and hearing it again brought back memories.

They'd rehearsed her lines in the tree house in her folks' backyard. At one point he'd almost kissed her, but only because the script called for it, of course. Then they'd both decided the kiss wasn't necessary for her to learn the part. He'd been relieved, of course, because kissing Tess would seem weird. But at the time he'd kind of wanted to try it, anyway.

"Aye, and it's a fine mornin', lass," he said. She looked great, as always, but there was something different about her this morning. He studied her, trying to figure it out. "Did you cut your hair?"

"Not since the last time you saw me." She used her fingers to comb it away from her face. "Why, does it look bad?"

"No. It looks fine." In twenty-three years of watching Tess create new looks with her thick brown hair, he'd lived through braids, kinky perms, supershort cuts, even red streaks. Once he'd given her a haircut himself after she got bubble gum stuck in it. Neither set of parents had been impressed with his barbering skills. He liked the way she wore it now, chin-length and simple, allowing her natural wave to show.

"Is there a spot on my shirt or something?" She glanced down at the old Copperville Miners T-shirt she wore.

"Nope." He nudged his hat to the back of his head with his thumb. "But I swear something's different about you." He stepped closer and took her chin in his hand. "Are you wearing some of that fancy department-store makeup?"

"To go riding? Now that would be stupid, wouldn't it?"

He gazed at her smooth skin and noticed that her freckles were in full view and her mouth was its normal pink color. Her eyelashes were soft and fluttery, not spiky the way they had been in high school when she'd caked on the mascara. Nope, no makeup.

But as he looked into her gray eyes, he figured out what was bothering him. They were best friends and didn't keep things from each other, or at least they hadn't until now. This morning, for whatever reason, Tess had a secret. It changed her whole expression, making her seem mysterious, almost sexy. Not that he ever thought of Tess as sexy. No way.

Despite himself, he was intrigued. Even a little excited. He didn't associate Tess with mystery, and it was a novel concept. He decided to wait and let the secret simmer in those big gray eyes of hers. It was fun to watch.

He tweaked her nose and stepped back. "I guess I'm seeing things. You're the same old Tess. Ready to mount up?" To his amazement, she blushed. Tess never blushed around him. They knew each other too well.

"Um, sure," she mumbled, heading straight for Peppermint Patty without looking at him, her cheeks still very pink. "We're burning daylight."

While he stood there trying to figure out what he'd said to make her blush, she climbed quickly into the saddle and started out. As he mounted he continued to watch her, and he could swear she shivered. With the temperature hovering around eighty-five on this June morning, he didn't think she was cold. This might be the most interesting morning ride he'd ever had with Tess.

MAYBE ASKING FOR Mac's help wouldn't be so simple, after all, Tess thought as she headed for the trail leading to the river. Here she was blushing over some offhand remark he'd made about *mounting up*. Or maybe she'd spent too much time reading *those* books, and every conversation had sexual overtones now. She certainly couldn't go to New York keyed up like this. It would be good to get this whole business over with.

Ducking an occasional overhanging mesquite branch, she rode at a trot ahead of him on the dusty trail. He knew something was up. She never could keep anything from him, so she might as well lay out her plan as soon as they got to their favorite spot by the river. As kids they'd used the sandy bank for fierce battles between their *Star Wars* action figures, and when they were older, they'd come out here to drink colas and talk about whatever was going on in their lives.

Tess had never shared the hideaway with anyone else, and neither had Mac, as far as she knew.

The riverbank was where they'd gone after Chewbacca died. They'd talked about heaven, and had decided horses had to be there or they weren't interested in going. They'd headed out here after Mac broke his arm and couldn't try out for Little League, and the day Tess had won a teddy bear at the school carnival. Before either of them knew anything about sex, they'd spent time by the river talking about whether men and women made babies the same way horses and dogs and goats did.

Later on, Mac had put a stop to their discussions on that topic. Now Tess wanted to reopen the discussion, but she wasn't sure if she had the courage.

"So what's your summer project this year?" Mac called up to her. "I know you always have one."

A perfect opening, but she didn't want to blurt it out while they were riding. "I'm still thinking about it." She drew confidence from the familiar rhythm of the little mare, the friendly squeak of saddle leather and the comfort of breathing in the dry, sweet air of early morning.

"Really? Hell, you usually have something planned by April. I'll never forget that summer you got hooked on Australia—you playing that god-awful didgeridoo while you made me cook shrimp on the barbie."

"How did I know it would spook the horses?"

Mac laughed. "The sound of that thing would spook a corpse. Do you ever play it anymore, or are you taking pity on your neighbors?"

"Watch yourself, or I'll be forced to remind you of the time you mooned my brothers."

"That was totally not my fault. You could have told

me the bridge club was coming out to admire your mom's roses."

Tess started to giggle. "So help me, I tried."

"Sure you did."

"The boys stopped me! I felt terrible that it happened."

"Uh-huh. That's why you busted a gut laughing and why you bring it up on a regular basis."

"Only in self-defense." She barely had to guide Peppermint Patty down the trail after all the times the horse had taken her to the river. The horses flushed a covey of quail as they trotted past.

She could smell the river ahead of them, and obviously so could Peppermint Patty. The mare picked up the pace. As always, Tess looked forward to her first glimpse of the miniature beach surrounded almost entirely by tall reeds. The perfect hideout.

As the mare reached the embankment and started down toward the sand, her hooves skidded a little on the loose dirt, but she maintained her balance, having years of experience on this particular slope. In front of them the river gurgled along, about fifty feet wide at this point. Other than a few ducks diving for breakfast and a mockingbird trilling away on a cottonwood branch across the river, the area was deserted.

There was no danger that anyone would overhear their discussion, and she trusted Mac to listen seriously without laughing as she laid out her problem and asked for his help. She couldn't have a better person in whom to place her confidence. Yet no matter how many times she told herself those things, her stomach clenched with nervousness.

MAC LET his gelding, Charlie Brown, pick his way down the embankment as Tess dismounted and led

Peppermint Patty over to the river for a drink. This morning was exactly like so many other mornings he and Tess had ridden down here, and yet he couldn't shake off the feeling that this morning was like no other they'd ever spent together.

He watered his horse, then took him over to the sycamore growing beside the river. He looped the reins around the same branch Tess had used to tie Peppermint Patty and went to sit beside Tess on a shady part of the riverbank.

He picked up a pebble and chucked it into the water. "Did you hear from that teacher at your new school?"

"Yep." Tess plucked a stem of dry grass and began shredding it between her fingers. "I got an e-mail from her and she'll be glad to let me stay with her until I can find an apartment."

Mac glanced at Tess. He'd wondered when she'd suggested the ride if she had something specific on her mind. Maybe this move had her spooked. She'd been renting a little house ever since she got the counselor's job at Copperville High, but living on her own in a small Arizona mining town with her parents three miles away was a lot different than living alone in New York City, two thousand miles from everyone she knew.

"Would this teacher rent you a room in her apartment?" he asked.

Tess shook her head. "She doesn't have the space. I'll be on the couch until I can find an apartment of my own. Besides, I want my own place. After growing up in a houseful of brothers, I've discovered I love the privacy of living alone."

"You just think you're living alone. Your family drops in on you all the time."

"I know." She sighed. "I love them, but I'm looking forward to being less convenient for a change."

Mac could understand that. It was one of the reasons he'd decided to get a private pilot's license. He looked for excuses to fly the Cessna because it was one of the few times he could be alone. "You might get lonesome," he said.

"I probably will." Tess began shredding another blade of wild grass. "But after living in a fishbowl for twenty-six years, lonesome doesn't sound so bad."

"Yeah." Mac tossed another pebble in the water. "I hear you." He breathed in the familiar mixture of scents—the dankness of the river, the sweetness of the grass, the light, flowery cologne Tess had worn for years, and the wash-line smell of sun on denim. Dammit all, he was going to miss her. He'd avoided facing that unpleasant fact ever since he found out that she'd gotten the job, but now it hit him all of a sudden, and he didn't like it.

Tess had been part of his world for as long as he could remember. So had the rest of her family, giving him the brothers and sister he'd always longed for. But Tess had always been the one he'd felt closest to. Maybe it was all those Halloweens together when she'd insisted he be Raggedy Andy to her Raggedy Ann, Han Solo to her Princess Leia, Superman to her Lois Lane. Or maybe it was the Easter-egg hunts, or the Monopoly games that lasted for days, or tag football— Tess had been there for everything. Every Christmas she dragged him out to go caroling even though he couldn't carry a tune in a bucket.

He'd die before admitting to her how much he'd

miss her. In the first place, they'd never been mushy and sentimental with each other, and in the second place, he didn't want to be a spoilsport right when she had this exciting chapter opening in her life. He was happy for her. He was jealous as hell and he'd have a hard time adjusting to her being gone, but that didn't mean he wasn't glad she had this chance.

"I'm glad you got the job," he said.

"Me, too. But I asked you to come here with me because I have this one problem, and I think you can help me."

"Sure. Anything."

"It's a different world there in New York, and I don't feel exactly...ready for it."

Her voice sounded funny as if she was having trouble getting the words out.

"You're ready." He broke off a blade of grass and chewed on the end of it. "You've been working up to this all your life. I've always known you'd go out there and do something special." He turned to her. "It's your ultimate quest, Tess. You might have butterflies, but you'll be great."

"Thanks." She smiled, but she looked preoccupied and very nervous.

He hoped she wasn't about to break their code and get sentimental. Sure, they wouldn't be able to see each other much, but they'd survive it.

She cleared her throat and turned to stare straight ahead at the river, concentrating on the water as if she'd never seen it flow before. God, he hoped she wouldn't start crying. She wasn't a crier, for which he'd always been grateful. He'd only see her cry a couple of times—when Chewbacca died and when that sleaze Bobby Hitchcock dumped her right before the senior prom. Good thing he hadn't had a date that night and had been able to fill in.

They'd had a terrific time, and he'd even considered asking her out again, for real. She'd looked so beautiful in her daffodil-yellow dress that it had made his throat tight, and to his surprise he'd been a little turned on by her when they'd danced. He'd almost kissed her on the dance floor, until he'd come to his senses and realized how that would be received by the Blakely brothers. Then, too, he might gross himself out, kissing a girl who was practically his sister.

She continued to gaze at the river. "Mac, I—"

"Hey, me, too," he said, desperate to stave off whatever sappy thing she might be about to say. If she got started down that road, no telling what sort of blubbering he'd do himself. He chewed more vigorously on the blade of grass.

"Oh, I don't think so," she said in a strained voice. "The thing is, Mac…I'm still a virgin."

In his surprise he spit the blade of grass clear into the river. Then he was taken with a fit of coughing that brought tears to his eyes.

She pounded him on the back, but the feel of her hand on him only made him cough harder. Ever since he'd discovered the wonders of sex, he'd made sure that he and Tess didn't talk about the subject. Life was a lot safer that way, and he wished to hell she hadn't decided to confess her situation to him this morning.

As he sat there wondering if he'd choke to death, she stood up and walked toward the river. Taking off her hat, she scooped water into it and brought it back to him. She held it in front of his nose. "Drink this."

He drank and then he took off his hat and poured the rest of the cool water over his head. As he shook the moisture from his eyes and drew in a deep breath, he felt marginally better.

She remained crouched in front of him, and he finally found the courage to look at her. "So what?" he said hoarsely.

"I'm *twenty-six years old.*"

"So?" His response lacked imagination, but she'd short-circuited his brain. If he'd ever thought about this, which he'd been careful not to, he'd have figured out that she was probably still a virgin. The Blakely boys had fenced her in from the day she'd entered puberty.

"I can't go to the big city like this. I can't counsel girls who've been sexually active since they were twelve if I've never, ever—"

"I get the picture." Much too graphically for his tastes. His mind had leaped ahead to a horrible possibility—that she would ask *him* to take care of her problem. And the horrible part was that he felt an urge stirring in him to grant her request. He pushed away the traitorous thought. "I think you could certainly go to New York without...experience. Chastity's catching on these days. You could be a role model."

"Oh, Mac! I don't want to be a role model for chastity! I didn't choose to be a virgin because of some deeply held belief. You know as well as I do that my brothers are the whole reason I'm in this fix."

Her brothers. God, they would skin him alive if he so much as laid a finger on her. "Well, your brothers aren't going to New York!" He knew the minute he said it that he'd stepped from the frying pan into the fire.

"No, they're not. And that's another point. I'll be clueless about sex and unchaperoned in a city full of sophisticated men. Is that what you want for me, to be swept off my feet by some fast-talking city slicker who'll play me for a fool because I don't know the score?"

This was a trap made in hell. And damned if he wasn't tempted. "Of course not, but—"

"I need a nice man, Mac. Somebody who can take care of this problem for me before I leave."

Oh, God. She was going to ask him. His heart hammered as he wondered if he'd have the strength to refuse her. "Listen, Tess. You don't know what you're saying."

"I know exactly what I'm saying. And you're the only person I trust to help me find that man."

2

"ARE YOU CRAZY?" Mac leaped to his feet so fast he knocked Tess over. The only thing worse than imagining *him* involved in this dirty deed was imagining *some other guy* involved. "Sorry." He reached down and gave her a hand up. Once she was steady on her feet, he released her hand quickly.

She dusted off the seat of her jeans. "Mac, please. I can't stay a virgin forever."

"Why not?" So he was being unreasonable. He couldn't help it. And dammit, now he'd caught himself watching her dust off her fanny and thinking that it was a very nice fanny. *Dammit.*

She sighed and lowered her head. "I was so counting on your help."

"Aw, jeez." Not only was he having inappropriate thoughts about her, he also felt as if he'd abandoned her. But he couldn't imagine how in hell he could diffuse either situation. "Tess, you know I'd do anything in the world for you, but I can't see how this would work."

Her head came up, and hope gleamed in her gray eyes.

He backed a step away from her. "Don't look at me like that."

"Here's how it will work. We'll brainstorm the possibilities and come up with a shortlist. Then you can find out if any of the guys are seeing anyone, because I don't want to break up any—"

"Whoa." Panic gripped him. "I never said I'd do this."

"You said you'd do anything for me."

"Anything but find you a lover!" Just saying it gave him the shivers. He'd worked so hard to keep from thinking of Tess in a sexual way, and now the barriers were coming down. For the first time he acknowledged the sweet stretch of her T-shirt across her breasts and the inviting curve of her hips. "I think that's a little more than a reasonable person should expect, don't you?"

"This is perfectly reasonable! Why should I search around on my own and end up with some clumsy nerdling who makes my first experience a nightmare, when I can rely on your advice and have a really nice time instead?"

There had to be a good answer to that one. He just needed a moment to think of it. And he couldn't think while he was picturing Tess having a "really nice time."

"See?" She gave him the superior little smile that she reserved for the times she'd won either an argument or a game of Monopoly. "You have to admit it makes sense."

"I don't have to admit anything. And why me? Why not one of your girlfriends? I thought women exchanged notes on guys all the time."

"They do, but you're a better source of info." She stuck her hands in her hip pockets. "You've dated more people around here than anyone I know. You'd know what women say about a guy, and you've had a chance to get to know the guys themselves and what they're really like. You'd know if they brag in the locker room, for example. Besides all that, there's not a single person, man or woman, I trust to keep my secret as much as I trust you."

He gulped. When she put it that way, he didn't know how he could refuse. And he wished she wouldn't stand like that, with her hands in her hip pockets and her chest thrust forward. He didn't like it. Okay, he liked it too much.

"Mac." She reached out and put her hand on his arm.

He tried not to flinch. Tess had put her hand on his arm a million times. She'd grabbed him for various reasons, usually to inflict injury, and he'd grabbed her back. He'd held her hand when she was a little kid and they'd gone trick-or-treating, and they'd clutched each other and screamed when they rode the Twister at the state fair. Touching had never been a big deal. Until now.

"Listen, Mac," she said. "You pulled out my first tooth, remember?"

"Different case."

"And you taught me to drive." She grinned. "You also gave me my first drink of whisky."

"You begged me for it, and then you threw up."

"And you held my head. You see, at all those important moments in my life, you were there to guide me."

"This is *way* different."

"Not if you stop being a prude."

"I'm not a—"

"What about Donny?"

"Donny Beauford?" He snorted. "You can't be serious."

"Why? What's wrong with Donny?"

Mac couldn't say exactly, except that when he thought of Donny in an intimate embrace with Tess, his skin began to crawl. He passed a hand over his face and gazed up through the leaves of the sycamore. Finally he glanced at her. "He wouldn't...take care of you."

"Oh." Her cheeks grew pink, but she faced him bravely. "You mean sexually?"

"In any way."

"Oh. Now, see, that's exactly what I need to know. How about Stu?"

"Oh, God, he's worse."

"Buck?"

"Nope."

"I know who. Jerry."

"Definitely not! Jerry's a dweeb. He'd probably—" Mac thought of some raunchy revelations he'd been privy to and decided to censor them. "Never mind. Not Jerry."

"Okay, then you make a suggestion."

He gazed at her as the silence filled with the sound of the river and the shuffling hooves of Peppermint Patty and Charlie Brown. The horses were becoming restless in the growing heat. Moisture trickled down his back, but he didn't think it was only the weather making him sweat. "I can't think of anybody." The truth was, he didn't want to think of anybody.

"Maybe you just need some time. I caught you by surprise."

"You certainly did that."

"Tell you what. Let's postpone the discussion. Maybe we could meet for dinner tonight."

"It's poker night."

"You're right. I can't, either. I'm playing pinochle at Joan's. Okay, then tomorrow night."

He decided a delay was the best he could hope for. He couldn't imagine what would occur to him to get him out of this mess in thirty-six hours, but maybe he'd stumble onto a miracle. "I'll meet you at the Nugget Café." He smiled. "It's meat-loaf night." Meat-loaf night at the Nugget was one of their shared treats.

"So it is. About six?"

"Yeah. Sounds good." He glanced up at the sun. "It's late. We'd better get back. I've got tons to do today."

"Yeah, me, too."

"Like what?"

"Research. I bought some books in Phoenix."

Mac had a feeling he shouldn't ask the question, but he did, anyway. "What sort of books?"

"On sexual techniques. When the time comes, I want to make sure I know as much as possible."

He felt as if somebody had kicked him in the stomach. "*This* is your summer project?"

"As a matter of fact, it is."

Mac groaned. It was even worse than he'd thought. When Tess settled on a summer project, a truckload of dynamite wouldn't dislodge her from her chosen path. If he knew Tess, and he thought he did, she would not be a virgin by the end of the summer. He could help her or not, but she would persevere until she'd checked off everything on her list.

TESS REALIZED how lucky she was that she liked each of the women her brothers had chosen to marry, and they liked her. When the guys got together for poker every Wednesday night, the wives hired baby-sitters and met at one of the other brothers' houses for pinochle. Tess was always invited. She'd miss the friendly, raucous evenings when she went to New York, but some sacrifices had to be made if she planned to live up to her own expectations.

Tonight the women were meeting at Rhino and Joan's. Rhino, originally named Ryan but indelibly stamped with a macho nickname in high school, was Tess's oldest brother and the acknowledged leader of the five siblings. He'd been the first to get married, buy a house and have kids.

From the moment Tess's niece Sarah had arrived in the world, Tess had decided being an aunt was the coolest thing in the world, although she was a little tired of being a maiden aunt. She arrived at Joan's early so she could see Sarah, who was now eight, and six-year-old Joe before Joan tucked them into bed.

After giving each of the kids the game she'd bought for them in Phoenix and joining in as Joan sang them silly good-night songs, she followed her dark-haired sister-in-law downstairs to the kitchen to help her get out chips and drinks for the party.

"Thanks for bringing them the game," Joan said as she took glasses out of the cupboard. "They're really going to miss you when you go to New York."

"I'm going to miss them." Tess emptied tortilla chips into a bowl and opened the refrigerator to search for the homemade salsa Joan always kept on hand.

"Oh, I don't know. You'll be living such an exciting life, I don't know if you'll miss anything from back here."

"Sure I will. I love this place, and my family and friends."

"Me, too." Joan turned to look at her. "But I'd give anything to be in your shoes."

"Really?" Tess gazed at her sister-in-law. With Joan's Hispanic, family-oriented background and her obvious dedication to her home and children, she seemed to have found her dream. "I thought you were the original Earth Mother."

"Don't get me wrong. I'm very happy. But the challenge has gone. When we first got married, everything was new. Sex was new, and then having kids was new, and then buying this house and fixing it up was new. But now it's all just a comfortable routine. And I want—" she paused to laugh "—more worlds to conquer, I guess."

"I so understand. That's the whole reason I'm going to New York. It's my Mount Everest." She hesitated, then decided to risk a suggestion. "Have you thought of going back to school?"

"I've already got the catalogs. I'm thinking—now don't laugh—of becoming a marriage counselor."

"No kidding! Joan, that would be wonderful. Obviously you know what goes into making a good marriage."

Joan gave her a rueful glance. "I wouldn't call me an expert. But I understand what happens when a couple gets to this point and sort of loses interest in each other."

Tess's jaw dropped. "You mean…"

"I mean things are getting really dull in the bedroom. I've been thinking of driving to Phoenix and getting some how-to books. I wouldn't dare buy anything like that in Copperville or the whole town would think I'd become a nymphomaniac."

"Amen to that. You know, I—" Tess stopped herself

before she offered Joan a couple of her research books. She loved and trusted Joan, but she wasn't quite ready to tell her sister-in-law about her summer project. "I think that's a good idea," she said.

"I figured you would. Listen, I'm not saying anything against your brother. He's a great guy. It's just that we could probably both use some pointers."

"Sure. Most people can."

"I mean, you know how it is. You get used to a certain way of doing things, and then it all becomes mechanical."

"Absolutely." Tess felt like an impostor, having this discussion with Joan, who assumed Tess had some experience. If she needed any further proof she was doing the right thing, here it was.

Joan came over and gave her a hug. "Thanks for listening and encouraging me. Even though you're younger than I am, I always think of you as being more sophisticated, for some reason. Maybe it's your college degree."

Tess returned the hug. "Book learning isn't everything."

"No." Joan stepped back and smiled at her. "The ideal thing would be to have both."

"I couldn't agree more." And if Mac would help her, she would have both, at last.

THE POKER GAME was held at Tiny Tim's, the youngest and the largest of the Blakely clan. Tim was a newlywed, proud to show off the new digs he shared with Suzie in an apartment complex near the edge of town.

Mac had spent the entire day worrying the subject of Tess's virginity, and the hell of it was, he could see her point. Her small-town background might make her seem unsophisticated to native New Yorkers. And if the kids she was counseling found out she had no sexual experience, either, that might become a credibility issue. Then there was the other problem—the very good possibility that some city dude, some fast-talking greenhorn, would take her virginity. Mac *really* didn't like thinking about that.

"Hey, Big Mac, are you in or not?" called Rhino from across the poker table.

Mac's head came up with a snap. Then he realized the question had to do with the cards in his hand, not whether he would help Tess find a lover for the summer. She'd sure ruined him for poker night. One of the things he loved about these weekly games was the simplicity of them. But nothing was simple tonight. No question was innocent. Even the name of the game, five card stud, had overtones he'd never noticed before.

He tossed his hand facedown on the table. "I'm out."

"Let's see what you got, Rhino," said Dozer, whose given name was Doug. Nobody called any of the brothers by their real names anymore. Doug and Hamilton, the two middle boys, had become Dozer and Hammer when they'd formed the heart of the offensive line for the Copperville High Miners.

The brothers were Mac's closest buddies, not counting Tess. Their mother and his were best friends, so the kids had naturally grown up spending a lot of time together. In high school the Blakely boys had literally covered his ass when he quarterbacked the Miners. But he saw them with new eyes tonight as he evaluated how each of them might react if they learned about the conversation he'd had with Tess this morning, and the fact that he hadn't turned her down flat.

"Read 'em and weep, Dozer," Rhino said, laying out two queens and three sevens. At the tender age of thirty he was starting to lose his hair, and so he wore baseball caps a lot, even inside. Tonight's was a black one from the Nugget Café.

Rhino didn't miss much, which made him a damn good poker player. He'd likely be the first one to figure out if Mac had lined up some guy to initiate Tess, and he'd probably organize the retaliation against Mac and the poor unfortunate guy Mac had brought into the picture.

"Aw, hell," muttered Dozer, a redhead with a temper to match. He acted first, thought about it later. He'd been known to deck a guy who so much as looked at Tess wrong. "You must be living right."

"Nah," said Tiny Tim, pushing back his chair. "He's ornery as ever. Just lucky. Who needs a beer?" Tim didn't have a mean bone in his huge body, and couldn't even go hunting because of his tender heart. He'd do anything for anybody and never took offense—except when it came to somebody bothering his sister. Then all his tenderness evaporated. Mac had seen it happen.

"Hit me," said Rhino with a tug on his cap. "And don't be bringing out any of that light crap, either."

"Yeah, he wants something to put hair on his head," said Dozer.

"Funny," said Rhino. "Real funny."

"Don't blame me for the light beer," said Tim as he headed for the kitchen. "Suzie bought it. Said I needed to watch my waistline."

"Yeah, Deena's been giving me that old song and dance, too," said Hammer, the third and smallest of the brothers, although at six-three he was no midget.

He was Mac's age and they'd been in many of the same classes in school. Logically he should have been Mac's best friend in the family, but Hammer wasn't a thinker, and Mac had always found more to talk about with Tess. Mac had often suspected Hammer was a little jealous of Mac's special relationship with his sister. This new development could really set him off.

Hammer glanced at Mac. "You don't know how good you've got it, with no woman to nag you to death about your diet."

"That's the truth," added Dozer. "It's getting so bad that if I haul out a bag of chips for *Monday Night Football*, Cindy tries to grab them away."

"And you let her?" Rhino asked. "You wouldn't catch that happening in my house. I lay down the law with Joan."

Mac led the chorus of hooting laughter. "Are you kidding?" he said. "Joan's got you wrapped around her little finger!"

Rhino grinned sheepishly.

"In fact," Mac continued, "I've never seen guys crazier about marriage than you four. You could hardly wait to march down that aisle. Don't give me this bull about nagging wives. You love every minute of it." And he envied them, he realized. They'd all found happiness.

Rhino took the beer Tim handed him and popped the tab. "So when are you gonna round out this ugly bunch and make it five for five?" He watched Mac over the rim of the can as he took a drink.

Mac gave his standard answer. "When I find the right woman."

"Hell, you've had a passel of right women." Dozer brushed back a lock of red hair from his forehead.

"Jenny was great. I dated Jenny, and there was nothing wrong with her."

"So why did you end up with Cindy?" Mac asked.

"Cindy knows how to handle my temper. But you don't have much of a temper, Mac. Jenny would've been fine for you."

"Yeah, she would," said Hammer. "Cute figure."

"Obviously I should have taken a poll before I broke up with her." Mac picked up his beer.

"And Babs," Rhino said. "I liked Babs, too."

Mac swallowed his beer. "Me, too. Just not enough to last forever."

"Aw, you're too picky, Mac," said Tiny Tim. "That's your problem. Nobody's gonna be perfect." He grinned. "Although Suzie's close." He ducked a shower of peanut shells.

"The newlywed nerd might have a point, though," Rhino said. "Maybe you are too damn picky. What kind of standards are you using, if you eliminated two nice girls like Jenny and Babs?"

Mac shelled a peanut and tossed it in his mouth. Then he glanced around the table. "You know, I'm truly touched that you all are so worried about my marriage prospects. Maybe we should hold hands and pray about it. Maybe, if we concentrate real hard, I'll see the light, and grab the next available female I run across."

Rhino's bushy eyebrows lifted and he glanced at Tiny Tim. "Seems to me this apartment complex has a pool."

"Sure does." Tim pushed back his chair, as did the other Blakely brothers.

Mac saw the look in their eyes and pushed back his

chair, too. "Now don't get hasty, guys. I was just making a joke."

"So are we," said Hammer. "Right, Dozer?"

"Yeah." Dozer grinned, revealing the tooth he'd chipped in the state championship football game eleven years earlier. "I *love* jokes."

As he was carried unceremoniously out to the pool and thrown in, Mac thought he probably deserved a dunking, but not for the reason the guys were doing it.

3

TESS HADN'T SPENT much of her life in dresses, but tonight's dinner with Mac seemed to require one. She didn't want to wear anything too fussy, not when the late-afternoon temperature had topped out at a hundred and five. She ended up choosing a sundress with daisies on it because she knew Mac liked daisies.

As she stood in front of the mirror wondering if she needed jewelry, she remembered the single teardrop pearl on a gold chain that Mac had given her as a high school graduation present. She'd been touched that he'd bought something so delicate and feminine, considering the rough-and-tumble nature of their friendship. Because she saved the necklace for special occasions, she seldom took it out of the black velvet box it had come in. Tonight seemed like the perfect time to wear it.

Once she was ready, apprehension hit her again. If Mac had willingly fallen in with her plan, she would have been calmer at this point. Her project was nerveracking enough even if Mac agreed to help. If he continued to drag his heels, she'd need to gather her self-confidence to stay on track.

Her rented bungalow wasn't far from the center of town, so she decided to walk the two blocks to the Nugget and work off some of her anxiety. She slipped on her sunglasses, hooked the strap of her purse over her shoulder and started out. A block into the walk, she knew she'd made a mistake. She'd arrive at the restaurant more cooked than the meat loaf.

Mac pulled into a parking spot in front of the Nugget as she passed the drugstore two doors down from the café. As she walked, she watched him climb out of his white pickup. Although the truck was dusty from a day spent on ranch work, Mac wasn't. He'd obviously changed into a clean shirt and jeans, and he was wearing a dove-gray Stetson she'd never seen on him before.

He looked damn good, with his cowboy-slim legs encased in crisp denim and his broad shoulders emphasized by the cut of his gray plaid western shirt. Every so often in the years they'd known each other, she'd paused to notice that her best friend was a hunk, but she hadn't done that lately. She was noticing it now.

Maybe all her reading was affecting her. She suddenly wondered what sort of lover *Mac* would be. Then she quickly put the thought out of her mind. Mac was like a fifth brother to her. She shouldn't be having such thoughts about him. He'd be horrified if he knew.

As if sensing her eyes on him, he glanced in her direction before going into the Nugget. He paused. "Did your car break down?"

"I decided to walk."

He scratched the back of his head as he stared at her. "But it's June."

"So I discovered. I have to admit I'm a little warm." Up close she could smell his aftershave and noticed there was no stubble on his square jaw. For some reason the fact that he'd showered and shaved for this dinner made her stomach fluttery.

He looked her up and down from behind his sunglasses and then shook his head. "I thought I taught you better than this. Now after that hot walk you'll hit that cold air-conditioning. It's not good for your system."

"Oh, for heaven's sake. You sound like my mother. Could you at least mention that my dress looks nice? I wore it because you like daisies."

"Your dress looks nice. And you're going to catch your death of cold in that restaurant."

It wasn't the reaction she'd expected. As her irritation grew, she realized she'd secretly hoped he'd be dazed and delighted by her appearance, the way guys in movies reacted when a tomboy type like her showed up in a dress. "Let me worry about that."

"Fine. Just don't come crying to me when you catch a summer cold."

"I promise it won't be your responsibility."

"I'm glad to know at least something's not my responsibility." He held the door open for her and the brass bells hanging from the handle jangled.

She stayed where she was. "Look, if that's going to be your attitude, maybe we should just forget the whole thing."

"And then what?"

"In or out, you two!" called Janice, a waitress who'd been working at the Nugget ever since Tess could remember. "We don't aim to air-condition the entire town of Copperville!"

Mac let the door swoosh closed again and turned back to Tess, his expression impassive. "What'll it be?"

She didn't really want to call the whole thing off. She needed Mac to help her, and besides, he'd shown up for dinner all shaved and showered. It would be a shame to waste that effort. "Let's have some meat loaf," she said.

MAC HELD THE DOOR for Tess a second time and tried not to drool as she walked past him trailing her cologne like a billowing scarf. When he'd seen her coming down the street in that flirty, daisy-covered dress he'd almost swallowed his tongue. Then she'd gotten close enough that he could see the moisture gathering in her cleavage, right where the pearl nestled.

He fought the crazy urge to lean down and lick the drop of moisture away before it disappeared into the valley between her breasts. He must be out of his mind. Fantasies like that didn't apply to Tess, the girl who could ride her bike no-hands down Suicide Hill, a girl who could throw a baseball so hard that it stung when it hit his glove. *But the girl is a woman now.* He couldn't ignore the truth any longer. He'd had glimpses of the fact over the years, like the first time he'd seen her in a bikini and she actually filled the thing out. And the prom had been another revelation, but he'd come to his senses before he'd done something stupid like kissing her. Sure they'd kissed when they were little kids, just to see what all the fuss was about, but it hadn't meant anything.

Funny, though, he still had a vivid memory of the spring day down by the river when they'd decided to try kissing. If he concentrated, he could still feel her soft little-girl's mouth that had tasted like pink bubble gum. When he'd pulled back to get her reaction, she'd looked sort of dreamy and sweet. Then she'd grinned at him and blown a big bubble that popped all over her face, destroying the moment.

He followed her through the restaurant to the back

booth, the one they always took at the Nugget. Along the way he managed to return greetings from the others in the café, people he'd known all his life. But his attention was claimed by the sway of Tess's hips under the flared skirt covered with daisies. The dress zipped in the back, and he figured she had nothing but panties on under it. The combination added up to what he and his buddies used to call a good makeout dress.

Damn. He had to stop thinking like this. Late this afternoon he'd finally decided maybe he should try to fix her up with someone. He'd come up with a couple of possibilities and had told himself he'd rather have Mitch or Randy be the lucky guy than some sleaze in New York.

Now he didn't want Mitch or Randy anywhere near her.

But if he didn't help her, no telling what harebrained thing she'd do. He'd seen her get a bee in her bonnet enough times to know she wouldn't give up her summer project easily. The year she'd decided to learn how to use in-line skates, she'd sprained her ankle and bloodied both knees, but she hadn't given up. And she had learned.

He slid into the booth across from her and tried to pretend this was like all the other times they'd shared a meal or a milk shake at the Nugget.

"Hungry?" she asked.

"You bet," he lied. He wondered if he'd be able to force anything down. He'd never look at her the same way again, he realized in despair. No matter what happened, the friendship had been changed forever. He'd made the mental leap and begun to think of her as a desirable woman—more desirable than he ever would have imagined. He could hardly believe that all these years he'd managed to screen out her sexuality.

"Have you been thinking about...what we discussed?"

"Some." He blew out a breath. "A lot."

"Any ideas?"

Yeah, and all of them X-rated.

Janice sauntered over to their table, notepad in hand. "Hey, you two."

Tess smiled at her. "Hey, Janice. How's that grandkid?"

Janice reached in the pocket of her skirt. "Take a look." She tossed a snapshot of a baby down on the table.

"Oh, Janice, she's gorgeous."

"Isn't she?"

"Cute kid," Mac said, although he was more interested in the look on Tess's face than the picture of Janice's grandchild. As Tess gazed at the photo, her expression grew soft and yearning. Only a fool would misinterpret that expression, and Mac wondered if Tess knew how much she wanted a baby of her own. Hell, that was another thing he'd never connected with Tess, but she'd make a great mother. Which meant she had to find somebody who'd be a great father. The whole idea depressed him.

Janice scooped the picture up and slipped it back in her pocket. "So, are you guys having meat loaf or something else?"

"Meat loaf for me," Tess said.

"Same here." Mac hoped he'd feel more like eating when their order arrived.

"The usual on the salad dressing?"

"Yep," they both said at once.

"Iced tea?"

"Yep," they said again.

Mac thought about Tess going to New York, where the waiters wouldn't automatically know she liked honey-mustard salad dressing, coffee in the winter and iced tea in the summer. He thought about her eating alone at a restaurant, or worse, eating with some guy. Some guy who would be having the same thoughts Mac was having right now.

"I'll be back with your tea and salads in a jiff." Janice headed back toward the kitchen.

Mac stared at Tess, not sure what to say for the first time in all the years he'd known her. They'd always been able to talk to each other. They'd been able to hang out without talking, too. She was the sort of girl you could take fishing, because she'd sit, her line in the water, and let the peacefulness of the day wash over her. But there was nothing peaceful in the silence between them tonight.

"It was pretty hot today," he said. Then he rolled his eyes. They'd been reduced to talking about the weather. "Forget I said that."

She smiled. "Okay." She leaned forward, which made the pearl shift and dip beneath the neckline of her dress. "Remember the time we put pennies on the train tracks?"

He gazed at the spot where the pearl had disappeared. Then he glanced up again, aware that he shouldn't be looking there. They were in a public place. Anyone could walk in and catch him at it. One of the Blakely boys, for example. "Yeah, I remember."

"I never told anybody."

"Me, neither."

"That was twenty years ago, Mac. You and I have

kept that silly secret for twenty years, because we both have the same sense of honor. That's why I'm asking you for help. I know you won't tell."

"I swear, you two look like you're hatching a plot," Janice said as she set down two iced teas, then plopped a salad plate in front of each of them and a basket of rolls in the center of the table. "Aren't you a little old to be painting water towers and such?"

"My folks' anniversary is coming up," Tess said. "Thirty-five years."

"Aha! And you're going to give them a surprise party."

Tess looked secretive. "Could be."

"My lips are zipped," Janice said. "But be sure and invite me."

"I will."

After she left, Mac leaned closer to Tess. The scent of her cologne worked on him, giving him ideas he shouldn't be having, but he didn't want anyone to overhear him. "You see how complicated this can get? Now you're going to have to give your parents a party to cover your tracks!"

She shrugged, and the straps of her dress moved. "No problem. It's a good idea, anyway."

His fingers tingled as he imagined slipping those straps down. Slipping the sundress down. With a soft oath he leaned back against the booth. "I'll bet you're freezing in here, right?" He wasn't freezing, that was for sure.

"Not really." She reached up with both hands and combed her damp hair back from her face with her fingers. The motion lifted her breasts under the cotton of the dress, and there was no doubt that she was braless. Mac told himself he wasn't getting turned on. Definitely not. "Let me get that old flannel shirt I keep in the truck."

"I don't need your old flannel shirt. I'm fine."

But he needed her to cover up. "I could get it anyway, just in case." He started to leave the booth.

"Mac, I don't want the blasted shirt, okay? I want to get this project going. So sit down and tell me what you've got."

He stared at her, his mind in turmoil. He should tell her about Mitch and Randy. He really should.

"Meat loaf's here!" Janice announced. "Goodness, you haven't touched your salads. Must be some party you two are cooking up."

"You don't know the half of it," Tess said. She moved her salad plate to one side. "Just set it down there, and I'll eat everything together."

"Me, too," Mac said, following suit.

"Better clean your plates," Janice said. "Or no dessert for you. And Sally made fresh peach pie today."

Mac patted his stomach, which was in no mood for a meal, let alone dessert. "Sounds great. You know I love peach."

Once Janice had disappeared, Tess leaned forward again. "That reminds me," she said in an undertone. "I've been learning the most amazing things from my reading. For example, the use of flavored oils. Did you know they make peach?"

"No." His jeans started growing tight. Mind over matter wasn't working.

"Have you read any books on the subject?"

"No." He stabbed his salad, determined to get through some of this food if it killed him.

"There are some wonderful ideas in there. You might want to take a look."

He lost control of his fork and it clattered to the plate. "I don't think so."

"Oh, for heaven's sake. Men and their egos. I'll bet even you could learn something."

He picked up his fork and returned to his meal with a vengeance. "Thanks, but I think I'll just blunder along on my own."

"Okay, but this is a perfect opportunity to check the books out without anybody knowing you're doing it. When I leave, I'll be taking those books with me and you'll be SOL."

"I won't be likely to forget you're leaving."

The light of amusement faded in her eyes. "Oh, Mac. I'm sorry. I didn't mean to say it like that. I know you'd love to do the same."

He clamped down on his emotions. There was no point in wanting what you couldn't have. "I wouldn't say that. And somebody has to take over the ranch. I noticed this past winter that my dad's already slowing down."

"Have you ever given them the slightest hint that you don't want to take over?"

"I do want to take over. They've struggled so hard to build that place and keep it going. It would kill them to have to sell it to strangers when they can't work it anymore." He looked into her eyes. "If you were an only child, would you be heading for New York?"

She seemed about to say yes, when she hesitated. Then she sighed. "Probably not. It really helps that my brothers look like they're going to stay in Copperville forever." She sent Mac a look of deep sympathy. "You can come and visit me anytime you want. I'll show you New York in style."

"Thanks. Maybe I'll take you up on that."

"We could have a great time. The top of the Empire State Building, the Statue of Liberty, Central Park, Times Square. Promise me that you'll come to visit me, Mac. It would be so wonderful to have that to look forward to."

"Okay, I promise." His heart wrenched at the thought of how much they probably would enjoy themselves. And then he'd have to come home again and leave her there. Well, he'd just have to get over it. His life was here, and hers would be there, and that's the way it was meant to be.

"I feel so much better, knowing that you'll come to visit me." Her eyes glowed. "I guess I always pictured seeing some of those things with you. Maybe I'll wait until you get there before I do some of that tourist stuff, so we can both experience it at the same time. I've heard Ellis Island is very moving. And the Metropolitan Museum of Art will be beautiful, and we could save our money and eat at one of those pricey restaurants, at least once, and—"

"I'm not taking you to a pricey restaurant unless you can do better on the food than you're doing here."

She glanced at her plate and picked up her fork. "I guess I'm distracted. I can't seem to think of anything except this move, and getting ready for it." She pushed her food around and glanced up at him. "Mac, I know you think I'm crazy for wanting this one thing before I go."

"Not crazy." He laid down his fork and gave up all pretense of eating. God, she was beautiful. Not cute, not attractive, not passable. Beautiful. He'd never admitted that to himself before, but he'd probably always known it on some unconscious level. He'd been entranced watching her talk about their future adventures in New York.

"Then you understand?"

"Yes."

She sagged against the table, and her sigh was heavy with relief. "Thank goodness. I wondered if I'd ever convince you."

"I'm convinced."

"Then you'll help me? You'll find someone and introduce us?"

Maybe he'd known all along what he had to do. Maybe he'd just needed time for the inescapable truth to settle upon him. But now he could see no other way. It was dangerous, extremely dangerous. A great deal was at stake. Still, it was the only answer, and he was man enough to accept that, along with the consequences.

He took a deep breath. "I don't have to look for someone. I already know who will do it."

"You do?" Her eyes grew bright, her cheeks pink. "Who?"

"Me."

4

TESS GASPED and put her hand over her mouth. She felt as if someone had dumped a bucket of warm water over her. Oh, God. Mac. Could she do it? Her imagination quivered and danced around the idea, unable to focus on the possibility. Her heart beat so loudly she thought he might be able to hear it. Mac. Oh, dear. How delicious. How impossible. How frightening. How lovely.

"Unless you don't want me to."

She was having trouble breathing, let alone talking. "I—I—"

"It's okay if you don't. I might not be...what you want."

"I...have to think."

"Sure."

Although she was caught up in her own turmoil, she sensed his vulnerability. "I'm honored," she choked out.

"*Honored?*"

"That you'd even consider...that you'd even be willing..."

"Better me than anybody else I can think of."

"Is it..." She paused and squeezed her eyes shut. "Such a sacrifice, then?" At his astonished laughter, she opened her eyes.

"Are you kidding?" He stared at her in wonder. "If

word got out that you were in the market, the line out-side your door would stretch all the way to the Nug-get."

"You think?" He'd never, ever given her such an ex-travagant compliment about her sex appeal. His com-pliments on that score had been nonexistent, come to think of it.

"You could have your pick," he said. "You don't have to settle for me. I just thought—"

"That I'd feel more comfortable with you. Thank you, Mac. And I probably would. Once I get over the shock."

"Take your time."

"You won't change your mind?"

He shook his head.

"But what about my brothers?"

He let out his breath in a great gust. "I won't pretend that won't be tough. But I've kept our secrets from them before." He gazed at her. "I guess I can do it again."

She'd never been so impressed with another human being in her life. "I don't deserve such a good friend."

He gave her a crooked smile. "Don't go giving me too much credit. This wouldn't be the worst assign-ment I'd ever drawn in my life."

"So you think you could have...fun?"

"I think I could manage that."

Tess leaned back in the booth and fanned herself with her hand. "Wow. This blows me away." She glanced at him with his fresh shower, shave and clothes. "Did you decide this before you showed up to-night?"

"No. I honestly didn't know what I was going to say to you when I got here. Then, while we were talking, I finally decided this was the only solution I could live with."

She hesitated, feeling unbelievably shy. "The reason I asked is that I wondered, considering that you're all cleaned up, if you thought that we'd just...take care of it."

He coughed and cleared his throat. "Is that what you want?"

She couldn't seem to control her racing pulse, and every breath was a struggle. "I don't know. I realize this is my project, but I'm not feeling very much in charge right now."

He gazed at her. "I have a suggestion."

She swallowed. He was the sexiest man she'd ever seen in her life. How had she missed that in all these years? "Okay."

He leaned forward and beckoned her to do the same. He lowered his voice and his eyes grew smoky blue. "Maybe we need to work up to this. We could take a drive, park somewhere, do some old-fashioned making out and see how it goes. And to take the pressure off, we'd agree not to go all the way this first time."

He was so close that his breath caressed her face. His hands—hands that had positioned her grip on a baseball bat, picked her up when she fell off her bike and pinched her when she'd dropped the frog down his back—had taken on a whole new significance. And they lay less than an inch from hers on the Formica tabletop. As she looked into his eyes, her heart beat so fast she thought she might have a heart attack. This was a Mac she'd never met before. "I g-guess we could do that, but..."

"But? And how were you envisioning the process?"

Her cheeks grew hot. "Honestly?"

"Honestly."

She kept her voice to a low murmur, which increased the sense of intimacy in the booth. "If you'd set me up with someone, I envisioned a one-night stand, to get it over with."

He winced. "That's a terrible idea."

"It is?"

He held her gaze with those electric eyes. "I thought you wanted to have a nice time."

"I do." She drew a shaky breath. "But couldn't I have a nice one-night stand?"

"Not you. Some women, maybe. Not you. You need to ease into it."

"That's why I've been reading all those books. And I'm a quick study."

His eyes twinkled and his mouth twitched as if he wanted to smile, but he didn't.

"What?"

"It's just so you, to thoroughly study a subject before you get into it."

He had her totally off balance, and she wasn't used to feeling that way with Mac. She tried to equalize the situation. "I could probably teach you a few things, Mr. Know-It-All!" she whispered a little louder than she'd meant to. Then she glanced around quickly to see if anyone was listening. Nobody seemed to be paying them any attention, which wasn't surprising. Seeing the two of them huddled over the table in the back booth of the Nugget was commonplace.

Mac leaned back against the worn seat, amusement in his eyes. "No doubt you could." As they continued to gaze at each other in silence, his expression became more guarded. He picked up his spoon and balanced it on his forefinger. "The question is, do you want to? Last time I checked, the ball was still in your court."

"I don't know, Mac. This is very...personal."

"That's a fact." He concentrated on the perfectly balanced spoon.

"You know me so well."

"About as well as anybody."

"Things would never be the same between us."

He laid the spoon down. "They're already different." He glanced at her. "Am I right?"

Oh, yes. The blue eyes she'd always taken for granted now had hidden secrets, and she was already wondering how those eyes would look filled with passion. Passion for her. The thought made her body tighten and throb in ways that had nothing to do with friendship. "You're right," she said.

"Let's get out of here."

Anticipation leaped in her, making her shiver. "What about your dinner?"

"I wasn't hungry to begin with. But if you want, we could have Janice box it up."

"Let's not bother. It won't last in this heat."

"Probably not." Mac reached in his back pocket for his wallet. "We don't need a bill. As long as we've been eating this Thursday-night special, we should know what it costs."

"Right." Tess opened her purse.

"Put your money away, Tess."

She glanced at him. "But we always split the bill. I don't want you to think that just because—"

"New game, new rules. You're my date tonight, and dinner's on me."

The gesture thrilled her more than she was willing to admit. "Aren't you taking this a little too literally?"

"Nope." He slid out of the booth. "I would expect any man in my position to have the courtesy to buy you a meal."

Her feminist conscience pricked her. "What, as some sort of barter arrangement?"

He took his hat from the hook at the end of the booth and settled it on his head. "No, as an expression of gratitude."

Her breath caught in her throat at his gallantry. No wonder he'd had women falling at his feet. She'd never quite understood it, but then, he'd never turned the full force of his charm on her.

Janice ambled over toward them. "Leaving so soon?" She glanced at their plates in surprise. "Was something wrong with the meat loaf?"

"No," Tess said. "We—"

"Goodness, you're flushed." Janice put her hand against Tess's cheek. "You're feeling feverish, child. I'll bet you're coming down with the flu."

"I think she might be, too," Mac said. "That's why we decided to leave."

"My Steve came down with the flu last week. You wouldn't think a bug could survive in this heat, but it seems to be going around. Best thing to do is stay in bed."

Tess felt her face heat, and she didn't dare meet Mac's gaze. "Right."

"Look at you!" Janice exclaimed. "You're burning up! Better get on home."

"What's wrong with Tess?" called Sam Donovan from his stool at the counter.

"Flu!" Janice called back.

"Flu?" asked Mabel Bellweather, popping up from the booth where she'd been sitting with her sister Florence. She hurried to Tess's side. "Should I call your mother, honey? She'd want to know if you've come down with the flu."

"I'll call her, Mrs. Bellweather," Mac said.

Mabel patted his arm. "You're a good boy, Jeremiah MacDougal. Anybody'd think you were kin to Tess, the way you've watched out for her over the years. I know she'll be in good hands."

Tess looked at the floor, at the walls covered with Frederic Remington prints, at the golden light of sunset outside the café windows. Anywhere but at Mac.

"Just get along now," Janice said, guiding them toward the door.

Although she wanted to run out the door, Tess made herself walk like a sick person as she preceded Mac through the restaurant. They exited to a chorus of get-well wishes.

Mac helped her into the truck. "Well, at least we're being inconspicuous about this."

"We can't go through with it," Tess wailed. "Soon everybody in town will know that you took me home from the Nugget, and—"

"And what?" He started the truck and switched on the air-conditioning. "You're letting a guilty conscience run away with you. They aren't the least bit suspicious of us being together." He backed out of the parking space and headed down the street toward her house.

"You're sure?"

"I'm sure. You saw the way Mrs. Bellweather patted me and told me I was a good boy."

Tess glanced over at him. "And is that what you intend to be?"

He pulled up at the town's only stoplight and gave

her a look that threatened to fry her circuits. "Depends on your definition."

STAY COOL, Mac told himself. He was supposed to be the experienced stud, the one who knew the score. If he gripped the wheel tightly enough, Tess wouldn't know that his hands were shaking. And if she noticed he was sweating, then he'd blame it on the hundred-degree temperature.

The reaction they'd gotten at the Nugget had convinced him of one thing—nobody would suspect that he and Tess had progressed to more than friends for the same reason he'd taken so long to come around to the idea. It was totally out of character for both of them. Even the Blakely brothers wouldn't guess, if he and Tess could keep from tipping them off.

But oh, God, what had he done? His whole world was turning upside down. If Tess agreed, then they would become lovers this summer, assuming he didn't turn out to be like his old dog George, who'd been taught to stay out of the living room when he was a puppy and now couldn't be dragged in there. Mac wasn't sure how deep his hands-off conditioning ran, but he might find out soon.

He'd already discovered he was more possessive about Tess than he'd ever dreamed. If he made love to her this summer, that possessiveness could get out of control. And he couldn't allow that, because she was going to New York, and she'd meet other guys there. And that would lead to...he didn't even want to think about where that would lead. He was setting himself up to go crazy, that's what he was doing.

But he couldn't see any other way around the problem.

"Are you really going to take me to my house?" she asked.

He glanced at her. She still hadn't committed to anything. "Do you want me to?"

"Not really." She was staring straight ahead, holding on to her little straw purse for dear life. Sunglasses hid her eyes, but her cheeks gave her away. They were the deep pink of the sunset lining the horizon. Her chest rose and fell quickly, making the pearl quiver in the valley where it lay against her golden skin.

The air in the cab grew sweet and thick with desire, until Mac felt as if he could lick it like a cone of soft-serve ice cream. "So you want to take that drive?" His voice was slightly hoarse.

"Yes, but I've figured out what we should do. Let's go to my house and sit in the driveway for a little while, in case anybody notices. Then I'll get down on the floor of the cab, and we can drive away to… wherever you had in mind."

Instantly he became aroused. Apparently the old dog would be able to learn new tricks. "All right."

She still didn't look at him. "You know, we might not be able to do anything. We might start laughing or something."

"Laughing's okay. Laughing usually means you're having a good time."

"I mean because we feel ridiculous."

That hadn't occurred to him. "Do you think you will? Feel ridiculous?"

"I don't know. Maybe I should pretend you're someone else."

"Don't do that." The idea incensed him more than it probably should have. "That would be insulting."

"Okay."

He pulled into her driveway and glanced at her. The pretending statement had him going. "Who would you pretend I was?"

"Nobody, because you don't want me to."

"Yeah, but if I didn't care, who would you superimpose over my face? Brad Pitt?"

She turned to him and took off her sunglasses. "I don't know. I hadn't really thought about it. Forget I said anything."

"Tom Cruise?"

"Mac, I won't be doing it, so let's drop the subject."

He couldn't drop it. He had to know who she thought was sexy. "Antonio Banderas? Mel Gibson?"

"All of them!" she said, clearly exasperated. "In a rotating sequence! With Leonardo DiCaprio thrown in for good measure! There, are you happy now?"

He stared at her. Good Lord, he was jealous that she'd imagine a movie star making love to her instead of him. He was in big trouble. "Sorry," he said. "Feel free to imagine anybody you want."

She looked at him as if he'd gone around the bend, which was pretty much true. "Okay."

"Just don't tell me about it."

"If you say so. But if you've never tried it, you might want to reconsider. Some men get very turned on by hearing their partner's fantasies about other men."

"Somehow I don't think I'd fall into that category."

"If you say so," she repeated. She seemed to be relaxing, if her superior little smile was any evidence. It was the kind of smile that told him she didn't think he had the foggiest notion what he was talking about.

Maybe he'd have to take a look at those books of hers, after all. She definitely had him at a disadvantage. Sure, he'd glanced through his share of sexy magazines when he was a teenager, but he'd been concentrating on the pictures, not the text. He'd thought he'd be the teacher and she, the student, the way it had been all their lives. The idea that she might know more about sex than he did wasn't entirely comfortable.

She unsnapped her seat belt. "I guess I'd better get down on the floor of the cab now," she said.

"Wait a minute. It's all dirty down there. You'll mess up your dress." He opened his door and reached around behind the seat where he always kept a soft blanket. He handed it to her. "Put that down first."

"I remember this! We used to make a tent with it in your backyard!"

"Yeah, that's the one."

She arranged it on the floor at her feet. "It's like meeting an old friend, seeing this blanket again, still so soft and blue. The binding's getting a little worn, though. What do you use it for, now?"

"Uh...different things." Suddenly he didn't want to tell her that he'd made love to several girls on that blanket. He kept it washed and tucked behind his seat to have handy if the weather was nice and the woman in his truck was willing. And now, dumb as it seemed, he felt as if he'd betrayed Tess by using the blanket that way.

She gazed at him. "It's all right, Mac. I know you've had a lot of women."

He shifted in his seat. "I wouldn't say I'd had a *lot*."

"Then my brothers must be lying. According to them, you've been to bed with more women than—"

"Does it matter?" He didn't like the direction the conversation was taking.

"I guess not. In a way it's a good thing. You've had

lots of experience, so I assume you'll know what to do."

"And what I don't know, you'll be able to teach me."

She looked at him, eyes narrowed. "You don't like that idea much, do you, Mac?"

Damn, but she could read him like a book. She was the only woman who'd ever been able to do that. "Hey, I'm always open to new things."

"I know you. You like to be the one who has all the answers."

"That's not true. I can take suggestions as well as the next man."

"The experts all warn that sex is a sensitive topic, especially for guys. Maybe it would be best if I didn't mention any of the things I've learned. I wouldn't want to give you a complex."

That did it. "A complex! Hell, woman, make all the damn suggestions you want! My ego can take it!"

"See? You're already upset."

"I am not upset!"

She always seemed to know when to stop arguing and just gaze at him quietly, reflecting his behavior back to him.

Finally he gave her a sheepish smile. "Okay, so I'm a little intimidated."

"Wouldn't you like to learn more, if you could?"

"Sure. Only a fool wouldn't."

"Good." She looked extremely pleased with herself. "Then I can contribute something, after all."

That made him grin. "You think your biggest contribution will be from a book?"

That seemed to shake her poise and she blushed bright red. "Well, um, I guess not."

"I guess not, either."

She met his gaze for a fraction longer before she glanced away, obviously rattled. She took a deep breath. "I'm scared to death, Mac."

"Even with me?"

She nodded. "Especially with you. I know you have high standards. What if I disappoint you?"

He reached out and took her hand. It was different from any other time he'd held her hand, and they both knew it. He waited until she turned her head and looked into his eyes. "I wouldn't have offered to do this if I didn't want to, Tess. There's no chance that I'll be disappointed."

The uncertainty eased in her gray eyes. "Thank you."

He squeezed her hand and released it. "We're giving each other the jitters, sitting here thinking about it. We'll be better off once we get started."

"You're probably right. So here goes." She turned on the seat and started hunching down so she could fit on the floor. "Take a look and make sure nobody's around to see me doing this."

He scanned the tidy little neighborhood. "I don't see anybody. Most people are probably inside having dinner right now."

She tucked herself down onto the blue blanket. "Punch it, cowboy."

And so it began. He took a deep breath and put the truck in Reverse. He'd done some wild things in his life, but this had to be the granddaddy of all risks he'd ever taken. He hoped that this time he hadn't finally bitten off more than he could chew.

5

KNEELING ON THE BLANKET on the floor of the truck, Tess felt more wild and crazy than she had in years. She had developed a taste for reckless adventure after tagging along after her brothers and Mac when she was a kid. Lately she'd been missing that adrenaline rush.

She rested her arms on the seat and pillowed her head on her arms. She had two choices—either she could look at the passenger-side door on her left or Mac's thigh on her right. With her feeling of adventure still running strong, she looked to her right.

His muscled thigh flexed as he stepped down on the gas, making the denim of his jeans move in subtle and tantalizing ways. Just beyond was the ridge of his fly. Her pulse quickened as she contemplated the ramifications of her decision. Of course, if they discovered they had no talent for making out with each other, they could call a halt to the whole program.

Mac clicked on the radio and a soft country tune filled the cab. She'd ridden in Mac's truck with the radio on hundreds of times. They'd sung along with the music, even rolled down the windows and turned up the volume when they were feeling really rowdy and wanted to stir up the neighborhood. She realized now that she'd always felt more alive when she was with Mac.

She certainly felt alive right now. Every nerve ending was checking in and registering the soft blanket under her knees, the tweed fabric of the seat beneath her arms, the waft of the air-conditioning over her bare back. The scent of Mac's aftershave used to be a comforting presence, letting her know her friend was nearby. Now it signaled something else entirely. The man who would soon take her in his arms was sitting very close to her.

"We're going to be on a dirt road in a minute," he said. "I'll try not to jolt you too much. Once we've gone a ways, you can probably sit up again."

"Where are we going?"

"A little road I found a couple of years ago. It goes out to the edge of a plateau where you have a nice view of Anvil Peak. Hold on. Here's comes the turnoff." He touched his booted foot to the brake, causing the denim to ripple again.

Watching Mac drive from this vantage point was quite an erotic experience, Tess decided.

He turned the wheel with one hand and reached over with the other to grip her shoulder as the truck bumped down off the pavement and onto the dirt. His hand was warm and sure as he held her steady. There was nothing seductive in his touch, and yet her heartbeat began to thunder in her ears and her whole body reacted to that point of contact. When he took his hand away, she wanted to have it back. Maybe his embrace wouldn't feel as awkward to her as she'd feared.

"Okay, I think you can sit up now. Nobody ever comes out here."

"Except you. You seem pretty familiar with the place." She crawled up to the seat and straightened her dress.

"I've been here a few times."

"Making out?"

"Now don't start asking me questions like that, Tess. You're going to spoil the mood for sure."

"Making out," she concluded.

He sighed and switched on the headlights.

"Well, I'm not dumb, you know. I understand the reason guys search for lonely roads." She looked around. Sure enough, there were no signs of civilization, just a road stretching to a point in the distance where the scrub-covered ground dropped away. Across the green swath of the river valley, Anvil Peak was silhouetted against a brick-red sky. To the right of that, the smokestack of the Arivaca Copper Mine sent a gentle plume into the air. "This is very pretty."

"I think so."

"So who did you bring out here?"

"Tess!"

"You pestered me about movie stars."

"And I shouldn't have. When two people are together, they should be concentrating on each other."

"Unless they want to explore the fantasy angle."

"Could we forget the fantasy angle? For all you know, being out here with you is my fantasy!"

She caught her breath and stared at him. "Is it?"

"No. Or at least I don't think so. I don't know what made me say that. Forget it."

But of course she couldn't forget it. And she remembered a dream she'd had about five years ago, one she'd put out of her mind as being silly. "Have you ever dreamed about me?"

"Of course I've dreamed about you. We see each other all the time. I dream about all the people in my life. Everybody does that."

"No, I mean, have you ever dreamed of me in a sexual way?"

He hesitated. "Yes. Once."

"So have I. About you."

He kept his attention on the dirt road. "That's probably normal."

"I didn't say it wasn't. What did you dream?"

"I…I can't remember."

"I don't believe you. Are you going to tell me what it was?"

"Nope."

"Do you want to know what I dreamed?" When he didn't answer, she smiled. "I'll take that as a yes. We'd gone out for ice cream at Creamy Cone one summer night, and mine was melting all over the place, and you'd forgotten to get napkins, like you always do."

"Not *always*."

"Most of the time. Anyway, I was a mess, and I didn't want to go home like that, so you decided the only solution was to lick the ice cream off me. We'd magically gotten down to the river by that time, and we were sitting on the sand in our special place. You started cleaning me up, like a cat would, and then…you started kissing me instead of licking, and…then you took my clothes off…" She wondered how much detail to include, but she felt dishonest leaving anything out.

"You kissed my breasts," she continued quickly, "and I said I was surprised you wanted to do that. You said you'd always wanted to, and you kissed them some more, and then you kissed me…all over." She decided to leave some details to his imagination. "Then right at the moment you were finally going to…well, you know…I woke up."

Her heart was pounding by the time she finished, and she had total recall of what she'd felt like in that dream, all warm and melting like the ice cream. She was definitely in the mood for a kiss. For more than a kiss.

Mac stopped the truck and switched off the lights and the engine. "That's...quite a dream." His voice sounded strained.

"Now you tell me yours."

"Maybe later."

"Was it anything like mine?"

"No."

She sat in the truck as the silence grew more and more intense between them. The air-conditioning was off, but the outside heat hadn't penetrated the cab yet. The warmth she felt was all coming from inside her, and she was ready to do something about it, but she didn't know whether she should make a move or let Mac be the first one. From the corner of her eye, she could see him sitting there, staring into space. He seemed hypnotized. At last she decided to say something. "What next?"

"Give me a minute. Then we'll take the blanket in the back."

She peered at him. "Are you feeling sick or something?"

"No, I'm feeling aroused."

"You *are*?" She glanced down at his jeans but it had become too dark to see much. "Cool. Was it my dream that turned you on?"

"Sure was. But then you probably knew that would happen, after all your reading about fantasies."

"No, I didn't." She felt thrilled with herself. "I wondered if you'd laugh."

He groaned. "I guess you don't know me as well as you think you do, then."

"Then you…really want me right now?"

He looked over at her. "Yeah. I really do. What a surprise, huh?"

"Oh, Mac." She put a hand against her racing heart. "That makes me feel so good."

He gave her a slow smile. "I guess this isn't going to be as difficult as we thought."

She smiled back. "I guess not. Want me to put the blanket in the back and wait for you?"

He took a deep breath. "I'm okay now."

"Are you ever going to tell me your dream?"

He took off his hat and laid it on the dash. "Not right now. It's a little more graphic than yours."

"And you said you didn't remember!"

"I've tried my damnedest to forget all about it. I thought I had, until you started talking about dreams." He opened his door. "Stay there. I'll come around and help you out. I don't want you stepping on a snake in those sandals."

"I've lived here all my life, Mac." She picked up the blanket from the floor. "I certainly know enough to check for snakes before I get out of a vehicle after dark in the middle of nowhere." She opened her door.

"Hey." He turned back to her. "Could you pretend that you're a timid female for a few minutes and give a guy a chance to be a big brave he-man? It's good for the ego."

"Oh." She grinned and pulled her door shut again. "All right, but I think it's stupid."

He shook his head. "Maybe this will be exactly as difficult as we thought."

Tess sat obediently while Mac rounded the truck

and opened her door, although waiting for him to take care of things wasn't her style. But if that made him feel more romantic, then she was all for it.

He held out his hand. "I'll take the blanket first and then come back for you."

"I can take the blanket."

"Tess."

"Oh, okay, here's the blanket, Mr. He-man, but this is dumb. We could make it in one trip."

"Yeah, if we're going for efficiency. I was after a different effect." He walked around to the back of the truck, pulled down the tailgate and climbed in.

She listened to him arranging the blanket. A couple of years ago, he'd installed an all-weather cushioned pad in the bed of his truck. At the time she'd wondered if it had anything to do with his love life, but she'd decided not to ask. Now she was pretty sure she knew the answer.

He hopped down from the truck and came back to where she was waiting.

"Can I put my dainty foot on the ground yet?" she asked.

"Not yet." He gazed up at her. "Have you ever been lifted down from a pickup?"

"Not since I was six years old. Once I could manage by myself, it seemed silly when I was perfectly capable of—*whoa!*" She gasped as he took her by the waist and lifted her out of the truck. Instinctively she put her arms on his shoulders, which was a good move because her feet still dangled in midair.

Balancing her against his chest and looking into her eyes, he let her slide down in a slow, sensuous movement. Warmth rushed through her as the friction of his body against hers gave her a complete and thoroughly arousing caress. At last her feet rested on the ground, and she let out her breath.

He held her close and gazed down at her. "Did that seem silly?"

Completely absorbed in the experience of being tucked so intimately against him, she shook her head.

"Think you're ready for a kiss?"

Oh. She gulped. "I...don't know."

"Let's try it." Holding her close with one arm, he reached up with his free hand and gently combed her hair back from her face.

She'd seen this tender side of him, usually when he was working around animals, or the times when she'd hurt herself and he'd been the one to doctor her up. But now she wasn't hurt, and his sensitive touch was meant to excite, not soothe her. He was succeeding admirably. She was trembling so much she wondered if she'd be able to stay upright.

"You're nervous."

"Yes."

"Me, too." He continued to comb her hair back, lightly massaging her scalp with his fingers.

"I can't tell." His touch felt awesome.

"Macho guys learn to hide their nerves. I'm hoping you like this."

"So am I."

He chuckled. "Do you remember the bubble-gum kiss?"

"Yes," she murmured. The more he stroked her hair, the less capable she felt of standing on her own.

"Did you like it?"

She took a shaky breath. "So much it scared me. So I started goofing around."

He began tracing the contours of her face with the tip

of his finger, ending with her mouth, which he out-
lined slowly and with great care. "I still remember how
your mouth felt that day."

She held as still as she could, considering the fine
quiver that seemed to have taken over her body. She
focused on his touch, wanting to record every subtle
variation in pressure.

He brushed her lower lip with his thumb. "Your
mouth is still as soft as it was then."

She gazed up at him, trying to make out his expression in the shadowy twilight.

He cradled her cheek. "The last time I touched you
like this, I was putting an ice pack over your eye, where
you got hit by a baseball."

She could barely see his smile in the darkness. "You
didn't touch me like this," she murmured.

"Sure I did." He slid his hand along her jaw and
leaned closer.

"No. You were rougher." Her heart thudded with
anticipation. "You were mad at me."

"I was mad at myself." He tilted her head back ever
so slightly. "I was the one who hit that ball."

"And I'm the one who bobbled it."

"Mmm. Your mouth looks sexy when you say *bobbled.*"

"You can't even see my mouth."

"Yes, I can. There's a little bit of light left over. That's
why I tilted your head back, to catch that light. I
wanted to see your mouth, to know I'm going to kiss it
soon. Say the word again."

Desire curled and stretched within her. "You're
crazy."

"Yeah." He drifted closer. "Say it for me, Tess."

"Bobbled."

"Again."

She felt his warm breath on her mouth. "Bobble—"

His lips touched hers, and in that instant, she knew that the world as she'd known it had ceased to exist. For she was really, truly kissing Mac, and now nothing would ever be the same.

TESS HAD BEEN forbidden fruit for so long that when Mac placed his mouth on hers, he half-expected a lightning bolt to strike him dead. Instead, her velvet lips welcomed him so completely that he drew back, his heart racing. Damn, this was going to be good. Too good. A man could lose himself to a kiss like that. If he'd ever secretly wondered if she was a virgin because she wasn't sensual, he'd been dead wrong. She was on fire.

"Mac?" she whispered. "Is something—"

With a groan he returned to her full mouth, committing himself to the kiss, to what would follow the kiss. To hell with what it might cost him. But he had a sinking feeling it would cost him more than he could ever guess.

For her mouth was a perfect fit for his. He didn't have to think about kissing Tess—it happened as effortlessly as breathing. She opened to him as if they'd been doing this for years, and although his body pounded with excitement, her invitation to pleasure seemed natural, almost expected. And he accepted without hesitation—tasting her richness, probing her heat, shifting the angle so he could deepen his quest.

Joy surged within him as she responded, pressing closer, moaning softly as he made love to her mouth. He thought of all the wasted years when she'd been there, only a touch away. But she was here now, so alive and warm in his arms, so ready.

Very ready. As she molded herself to him, he could feel her nipples, tight and aroused, pressing against his chest. His erection strained against his jeans. If he didn't slow down, he'd violate the terms of tonight's agreement and make love to her out here in the desert. That couldn't happen, first of all because he believed what he'd said about not rushing the process, and second because he had no birth control with him.

With great regret he drew back, breathing hard. The sun had gone down, and the stars didn't allow him to see her expression very well. He wished he could, but maybe it was for the best. Tonight promised to be intense enough without being able to see desire written all over her face.

"I...liked that," she said. Her breathing was about as ragged as his.

"Yeah." He rubbed her back and took a deep breath as a chorus of crickets started up in the nearby sagebrush. "Me, too."

She wound her arms around his neck and leaned back to look up at him, although she probably couldn't see his expression, either. "You're aroused again. I can tell by your voice."

"Any guy would be aroused if you kissed him like that."

"Was I too...uninhibited?" She sounded genuinely worried.

"God, no. You were great."

"I wondered, because I don't usually get so..." She paused. "Excited."

Man, he loved hearing that. "Really?"

"Especially the first time I kiss someone. You're, um,

very good at this kissing business. I guess it's all your practice that gives you such good technique."

"That wasn't technique." He loved running his fingers through her hair. "That was...I don't know. You inspired me, I guess."

"Oh." There was a world of self-satisfaction in that tiny syllable.

He began itching to kiss her again. And he had all the rest of the territory labeled as "making out" to enjoy. Even knowing he wouldn't have the ultimate experience tonight didn't dampen his enthusiasm for the next step. "Ready to climb in the back of the truck?"

"I've been thinking. Are you sure you should?"

He laughed. "I think we dispensed with that a while back. No, I probably shouldn't, but I will anyway, because it's still the best solution."

"No, I mean, with the way you react when we kiss. I'll bet you're not used to just making out with a woman and not finishing the job. You're liable to get awfully frustrated."

He grinned down at her. "So are you. That's the idea—to build up to the main event, so we're really ready for it."

"I can understand that strategy for me, because of my lack of experience, but I'm afraid I'll be torturing you. I know from my reading that some men are able to draw out foreplay for a very long time, but I'm sure they extend that time gradually, so their bodies are used to delayed gratification. You wouldn't be in that category."

He sorted through that little speech until he thought he understood. "Are you saying you're willing to sacrifice yourself for my benefit?"

"I...yes, I am. We don't have to stop with just making out if you find that you're too...uncomfortable."

Oh, God. Heaven was within reach and he'd been caught unprepared. He took a deep breath. "Well, as willing as you are to make the supreme sacrifice for me tonight, it won't be possible. I don't have birth control with me."

She met his declaration with stunned silence. "You don't?"

"Of course not. What, you think I carry a supply around with me at all times, just in case I get lucky?"

"Not even in your wallet?"

"Not since high school. These days I have a much better idea of what will and won't happen with a woman, and I plan accordingly."

She seemed to be digesting that. "What about in the glove compartment of your truck?" she finally asked.

"Are you kidding? My mom's been known to borrow my truck, and she's also been known to get a speeding ticket now and then. I can imagine how much she'd love finding condoms in the glove compartment when she's digging for the registration papers."

She gazed up at him. "You know, I'm glad to find out you don't keep some around at all times."

"You had me pegged as some sort of sex machine, didn't you?"

"Not exactly a machine, but everybody thinks you installed that spongy mat in the back of your truck so you could have fun with your girlfriends."

He let out a sigh of exasperation. "I put that mat in the back of the truck when Mom started refinishing antiques, so she could haul them around without damaging the finish on the furniture."

"Not for making love?"

"No."

"And so you've never—"

"I didn't say that. And this discussion's over." He swung her up in his arms before she traveled down that road any further. Of course he'd made love in the back of the truck, but he didn't want to talk about it now.

"What are you doing?"

"I'm taking charge and carrying you to the back of the truck. It's the manly thing to do." She didn't resist, so he concluded she had faith in his self-control. He was putting a huge amount of faith in it, himself.

"Then I guess you don't want to talk about your love life anymore," she said.

"You've got that right." Specifically he didn't want to talk about or think about any other women he'd been involved with, in the back of his truck or anywhere else. They'd been wrong for him, but he hadn't realized how wrong until a few moments ago...when he'd kissed Tess.

6

TESS SAT CROSS-LEGGED on the blanket and waited for Mac to crawl into the bed of the truck and join her. The night was still very warm, but she felt shivery with delight. Maybe it was partly the blanket, reminding her of the tent she'd shared with Mac as kids. They'd hauled comic books and snacks into their hideaway, and there had been nothing sexual about the cozy intimacy of being stretched out beside him in that tent.

Or maybe there had been, and she had been too innocent to realize it. At any rate, she had a delicious sensation now that reminded her of that intimacy, only magnified a hundred times. They were alone, closed off from the world, and ready, in a sense, to play.

"The sky's so clear," Mac said as he crawled up beside her. "Let's lie on our backs and look at the stars, like we used to."

"And not do anything?" She was hungrier for him than she cared to admit.

He gave her a swift kiss on the mouth. "I'll tell you my dream."

"Oh, all *right*." She pulled the skirt of her dress down underneath her as she settled back on the blanket and looked upward. "Big Dipper, Little Dipper, North Star," she said automatically as she searched them out.

Mac lay down beside her, his arm touching hers, his

thigh against hers. "Orion's Belt, and the Seven Sisters," he added.

"And?"

"And nothing. That's all I ever learned."

"Still? I thought you took an astronomy class."

"I learned things for the test and then forgot it. I only remember what we figured out from that kid's book you had on the constellations."

"Slacker."

"Yeah."

Tess felt as if they could still be seven and nine, lying on their backs in the cool grass of the park on a summer's night. Tess's brothers would be racing around playing tag, and the grown-ups would be sitting in lawn chairs complaining about being stuffed. Meanwhile, Mac and Tess would be off by themselves looking at the stars, probably because they'd been the ones most captivated by *Star Wars* and galaxies far, far away.

She could almost imagine they'd gone back in time...until Mac reached for her hand, lacing his fingers through hers. Memories of childhood faded. They definitely weren't kids anymore, and the emotions coursing through her at the barest touch of his hand weren't the least bit childish.

But the basis of those feelings had been there all along, she thought. What was happening between them now had been simmering within her for years, waiting for a touch, a word, a gesture, to make passion flare to life. He rubbed his thumb along hers, and although it might have been an unconscious movement, she didn't think so. He had to realize that what they'd taken for childhood play had been more sensual than they'd ever admitted to each other, or themselves.

"Tell me your dream," she said.

He was silent for a moment. Then, with a little sigh that sounded like surrender, he began. "You'd been invited to a Halloween party, and you asked to borrow Peppermint Patty because you wanted to go as Lady Godiva."

"*What?* I would never do such a thing." She thought of riding bareback with no clothes on. It didn't sound comfortable, but it was sort of erotic. "Did I have long hair?"

"Down to your hips. You wanted to practice riding with no clothes on to see how it felt before you tried it at the party, so you talked me into riding along the river trail with you. You rode bareback, and you had this loose dress on with nothing on underneath. Halfway along the trail you took off the dress and tossed it into the bushes."

Tess shivered. It *was* a sexy image. "But my hair covered me up, right?"

"Not that well. And you know how the trail winds, so even though I was behind you, I got some side views. You were…" He cleared his throat. "You were beautiful. And riding like that, rocking back and forth on the horse, was turning you on."

"How could you tell?"

"Your skin was flushed, and you were breathing faster, and…your nipples were hard." Mac clutched her hand a little more tightly and cleared his throat again.

"Oh." Which described exactly the way she was feeling right now. When Mac didn't continue with the dream, she prompted him. "Did you wake up then?"

"No."

"What happened?"

"You had an orgasm."

"Oh!"

"Which turned *me* on, and I pulled you off the horse and made love to you right on the ground."

Tess wasn't sure who was holding on tighter, her or Mac, but they had each other in a death grip. "Was it…nice?"

His voice was hoarse. "It was a dream. You can't put dreams up against the real thing."

Disappointment shot through her. "Then it wasn't nice."

"No, it wasn't nice. It was wild and primitive, no holds barred. I bit your neck and you dug your fingernails into my back. It was…fantastic."

"Wow." She wondered what he'd think if he knew how her body was throbbing this very minute. Being thrown to the ground and ravished sounded perfect. She loosened her grip when she realized she might already be digging her nails into his hand.

He released her hand and turned on his side to face her. "I don't want you to be scared by that description, Tess. I would never be that rough in real life."

She turned on her side, too, pillowing her head on her arm. But her casual posture belied her racing heart. "Too bad."

He sucked in his breath. "You'd *want* that?"

"Would I want you to be so overcome with desire that you'd pull me from my horse and make love to me on the ground? Of course I would. But as you said, it was a dream. In real life—"

"In real life I want you even more than that."

She gasped. "You *do?*"

He lifted a hand to her cheek, and as he caressed her, his hand trembled. "In real life, I want to rip that dress away and take you now, right now. But I won't. It wouldn't be fair to you."

"It would so be fair!"

His laugh sounded strained. "No, it wouldn't."

She'd never heard that edgy tone in his voice, and it was more exciting than the tenderest of murmurs. She almost wished he would be that reckless, but of course he wouldn't, which was why she was lying here with him now. She trusted him. "But taking it slow doesn't seem fair to *you*," she said.

He slid his hand to the nape of her neck, massaging gently. "Fair doesn't even come into it. I never imagined I'd be lying here with you like this. It's like getting a present I didn't have sense enough to know I wanted." He fingered the clasp of her necklace. "What made you decide to wear this tonight?"

"It seemed right."

"It was," he murmured. His lips found hers and his kiss soon brought her to a fever pitch.

She didn't realize he'd begun unzipping her dress until the material loosened over her breasts and he drew back slightly, gently ending the kiss. She opened her eyes. His face was in shadow, but she could see the rapid rise and fall of his chest as he eased the zipper the rest of the way down.

"Stop me whenever you want," he said in a husky voice.

"I don't want to stop you." Her heart pounded as the thin strap of her dress dropped from her shoulder.

"Just know that you can." He took the strap carefully between his fingers and pulled it down, bringing the bodice of the dress with it, gradually exposing her breast. His breath caught. "Oh, Tess." He eased her to her back and expertly drew the dress down to her waist. Then he groaned and shook his head.

"What are you thinking?"

"That you're even more beautiful than in my dream. And that you've been right there, all along...."

Her mouth moistened with desire. "All covered up."

"Yeah. Damn. All these years."

"Aren't you going to...touch me?"

"I'm still caught up in looking." But at last he traced the aureole of one nipple, causing it to tighten even more. Then he cupped her so tenderly, so carefully, that she felt like precious china. She loved being cherished, but she wanted more. Perhaps she needed to show him. Arching her back, she pressed forward, filling his cupped palm.

"Ah, Tess." Taking a shaky breath, he dipped his head and brought her tight, aching nipple into his mouth.

Yes. She cupped the back of his head and lifted into his caress. Oh, yes. His was the touch she'd been waiting for—the swirl of his tongue, the nip of his teeth, the sweet pressure as he sucked, nursing the flames that licked at the tender spot between her thighs. Shamelessly she offered her other breast, and he lavished the same loving attention there while continuing to give a sweet massage to the damp nipple he'd just left.

As she twisted on the soft blanket, her skirt rode up. Or maybe he pushed it up, in that subtle way he had of making her clothes disappear. He slipped his hand between her thighs, pressing against the damp silk of her panties. The heel of his hand found the spot that ached, and pushed down. She trembled.

He kissed his way back to her mouth, then lifted a

fraction away from her lips. "Do you want me to stop?"

"No," she said, panting. "But I don't…I've never…"

He paused, breathing heavily, too. "No man has ever had his hand there?"

"They didn't dare."

He leaned his forehead against hers. "But you must have done this…yourself."

"No, I—read about it."

"Not the same."

"I know but—promise not to laugh—I didn't want to be alone when it happened."

"Oh, sweetheart." He didn't laugh. Instead, he tenderly kissed her forehead, her nose, her cheeks, and finally her lips. "You're not alone now," he whispered between kisses.

And sometime in the midst of those bewitching kisses, he eased his hand beneath the waistband of her panties. When she felt his fingers slip through her damp curls, she gasped.

His hand stilled and he lifted his mouth away from hers. "Is that a no?"

She began to quiver and fought the urge to press her thighs together. His hand resting there felt wonderful, but frightening, too. "Just a…reaction."

"Should I stop?"

"No. But Mac, this is so personal."

"Yes, ma'am." There was a definite smile in his voice. "About as personal as you can get." He eased his hand down and began a slow massage.

Breathing became more difficult as her body responded to that easy stroke. "At least…it's almost completely dark."

"That can help. The first time."

She felt as if he was transforming her into a liquid, flowing state. "What if I make a fool of myself?"

"I hope you do."

"I hope I don't. You'll never let me forget it." She gasped again as one of his very talented fingers sought out the sensitive nub that sent shivers zinging through her.

"No, I probably won't," he murmured as he kept up the maddening, electrifying rhythm.

She felt like a watch being wound too tight, but she wanted him to keep on winding. "Oh, Mac." She clutched his shoulder as the tension grew.

"Won't be long now." He leaned down and feathered a kiss against her lips. "Let go, Tess."

"I don't know how."

"Your body knows. Get out of your head and live right…" He pressed down a little harder. "Right *there*."

She moaned as the pressure became unbearable and her body arched and quivered beneath him.

He leaned over and whispered in her ear as he deepened the caress. "Remember my dream? You rode naked to the river, becoming so aroused that you climaxed, and then I pulled you down, spread your legs and—"

She cried out as the convulsions swept through her, wave upon wave of glorious release. And all through it, she held on to Mac, the man who had offered to lead her into this land of magic, and then had made a miracle happen. And he held on to her equally as tight, covering her face with kisses and laughing softly in triumph.

MAC HELD Tess and listened with pride to her sighs of satisfaction as she nestled in his arms. He was tense with unfulfilled need, but he could stand the pressure. "So you liked it."

"I adored it." Her voice was lazy and sweet, an after-the-loving voice that didn't sound like the Tess he knew, but like a Tess he'd like to know. "Mac, you used fantasy on me, after all."

"Had to get you past that wall."

"See?" Her voice was whisper-soft. "Fantasy can work."

"You made a believer of me."

She sighed again. "I'm so glad you were the one, Mac."

"Me, too." Even when Tess had announced she was still a virgin, Mac had never dreamed that she'd never experienced what he'd just given her. Knowing that he'd introduced her to her first orgasm made him feel like a king. Of all the accomplishments in his life, this might be the one he was the most proud of.

On the downside, he was in real agony. Tess had been right that he was used to finishing something that started this way, and his body was demanding that he take care of things. Even without birth control, there were ways to gain mutual satisfaction. But she couldn't be expected to do that for him, considering her lack of experience. He wouldn't even ask.

Then he felt her fingers working at his belt buckle.

"Tess? What are you doing?"

"If you'd move back a little I could do it better." She fumbled her way through the fastenings of his button-fly jeans. It was obvious she'd never undressed a man in her life.

Suddenly he felt protective of her innocence. "Look, you're new at this, so please don't think that I expect you to—"

"Want me to stop?" She paused. "It's just that, in the dark, I feel...braver. And I want to, Mac. I really want to."

She'd nearly released him from the confines of the denim, which left only the cotton of his boxers between him and paradise. Consideration warred with urgent need. "Uh..."

"I'll confess I'm a complete novice when it comes to giving a man pleasure, but I've read extensively." Her words might be scholarly, but her tone was sexy as hell.

The combination of sex and innocence was dynamite. His erection stiffened even more, thinking of her untutored hands on him, practicing.

She rubbed him through the cotton. "Well?"

With a sigh, he kissed her deeply. "Considering it's dark and all, I'd love it," he murmured against her lips.

"Then lift your hips so I can push your clothes away. I'm too much of a beginner to deal with impediments."

His skin flushed with anticipation. He'd never in his life been approached this way, and he found it damn exciting. "Okay." He lifted up and she shoved his boxers and jeans down in one efficient movement.

"Goodness gracious." She sounded intimidated.

Well, at least he wasn't a disappointment to her. He took some satisfaction in that. "Change your mind?"

"No. I'm just...impressed. Lie back and let me get used to the idea."

He did, and realized he was quivering—like a first-timer. When she finally circled his shaft with one warm hand, he squeezed his eyes shut and gritted his teeth. He would not explode this very minute. He would not. Talk about making a fool of yourself. But even the thought of Tess holding on to him like that was enough to make him climax. The reality was so stimulating that he wondered how long he'd survive her attentions.

"Your skin here is so soft."

"Mmm."

"Let me just moisten it."

Before he realized what she was up to, she'd leaned down and started using her tongue. "Tess!"

She lifted her head. "Am I shocking you?"

"Yes! You're not ready for that stage yet."

"I'm not?" She moved her hand up and down his shaft. "Or you're not? Are you okay? Your face is all scrunched up."

"I'm trying to control myself. And when you do unexpected…things, I find it difficult."

"Oh. So you don't want this to be over too quick?"

"Right." He groaned as she settled into a rhythm that was uncannily good for someone who had never engaged in this activity. She must have some good books.

"Do you suffer from premature—"

"No!"

"Because there are techniques for that."

"Tess, I'm fine…usually." He clenched his jaw and fought the urge to erupt as she explored the tip of his penis with fluttering fingers. And he knew in a flash of certainty he was reacting this way because these were Tess's fingers touching him so intimately. "Maybe it's because I've wanted you for so long, without knowing."

"That's a nice thought." She leaned down and flicked her tongue back and forth against the spot she'd been caressing with her fingers.

He worked so hard to hold back his climax that he

thought he might pass out. "Where...did you learn that?"

"A book." She blew on the damp spot. "Do you like it?"

He gripped the blanket in both fists and stared blindly up at the night sky. He'd never had an experience to equal this one. "Yeah. I like it."

"Too bad we don't have some ice."

"*Ice?*" He definitely had to get a look at those books. "What—what for?"

"It's supposed to feel fantastic during an orgasm if you put some right here." She pressed against a spot below his family jewels.

He didn't know about ice, but the pressure she was exerting was having a fantastic effect. He moaned softly.

"Having trouble holding back?"

"Yeah, you could say that."

"Then let's try this." She held him snugly at the base of his shaft with one hand, pushing down slightly, and took the tip in her mouth.

The effect was unbelievable. Intense pleasure poured through him from the action of her mouth, but her firm grip on his shaft kept his climax at bay. He moaned. He groaned. He thrashed his head from side to side.

Then she released her grip, took him completely into her mouth, and his control shattered. He tried to pull away from her, sure this wasn't what she meant to do, but she wouldn't let him. His world came apart as he surrendered to the most cataclysmic orgasm of his life. As his spinning universe slowly came back into focus, he drew her up and gathered her close to kiss her passion-flavored lips.

He felt as if he'd been poleaxed. This evening had started out to be an educational session with him as teacher and her as pupil. Somehow, in the past few minutes, she'd completely reversed their roles. And in the process she'd made him her slave.

"We can try the ice another time," she whispered.

"Sure." He held her close, unable to find the energy to do more than breathe.

7

TESS HAD NEVER SEEN Mac so still, not even the time he rode all day without a hat and ended up with sunstroke. He was usually brimming with energy, yet he lay slumped against her like an unconscious person, his eyes closed. On the other hand, the experience of loving Mac had stirred her up again. She'd finally experienced activities she'd only read about, and she felt as if a whole new world had just opened up for her. She was ready for...more. She wasn't sure exactly what form that "more" would take, but she was ready for it.

She peered into his relaxed face. "Mac, I didn't hurt you, did I?"

His mouth curved in a faint smile. "Nope."

She stroked his hair back from his forehead. "You're awfully quiet."

His lips barely moved enough to form the words. "Your books should tell you why."

"It was that good?"

"Yeah, Tess, it was."

"Cool." She smiled to herself in the darkness. "I was wondering if I'd done everything right."

"Extremely right."

"Good." She adjusted her position. "Is it okay if I kiss you again?"

His eyes drifted open. "Where?"

"On your mouth. Where did you think?"

"I wasn't sure. For a virgin, you have some amazing ideas."

She brushed her lips against his. "I'll take that as a compliment."

"It was."

She settled her mouth over his, coaxing his tongue into slow love-play with hers. At first his response was lazy, almost nonchalant, but gradually the tempo of his breathing picked up. As the temperature of his kiss changed from warm to sizzling, he cupped her breast, kneading it with sure fingers. Her body throbbed with new knowledge, and she whimpered and moved closer to his heat.

He drew his mouth back a fraction. "Oh, Tess. I'm getting hard again."

She reached downward. "Let me—"

"No." He captured her hand. "We have to stop. I thought I was so drained that I could just play around for a while more without getting too worked up. I was wrong. I don't trust myself if we get started again."

Her body tightened in anticipation. "You'd ravish me?"

"There's a good chance." He reached for the strap of her dress. "Let's put this back on."

"Mac..." She could hardly believe that she was about to make such a bold suggestion, but she wanted this night to continue forever. "I'm sure you have birth control stashed somewhere at home. You could take me back to my house, go get it, and then come back to my place."

He paused in the act of pulling the bodice of her dress back up over her breasts.

"You see, I want you, too," she murmured.

He trembled and bunched the material in his fist.

"There's still a lot of time before the sun comes up."

He drew a long, shaky breath and continued his task, reaching for the zipper of her dress. "It's probably stupid, but I want to stick with what I promised you. You'll only have the experience of giving up your virginity once in your life. I think…we should make it special."

"We could make it special tonight."

"Not special enough. Give me a chance to woo you a little. Let me bring you flowers, maybe a bottle of good wine."

Despite her frustration, she liked the picture he was painting. "Should I buy lingerie or something?"

"Lingerie would be very nice." He arranged the pearl in the cleft between her breasts. "But wear this. I love watching the way it nestles right there."

"I'll bet when you gave it to me you never imagined a scene like this."

"Not consciously." He ran a finger over the gold chain. "But maybe subconsciously. When I saw the necklace in the jewelry store, I knew immediately I wanted to get it for you for graduation." He looked into her eyes. "Maybe I wanted something that would touch you where I wasn't allowed to."

She smiled. "We seem to have overcome those restrictions without too much trouble. I'd say our make-out session was a success."

"Yeah, but now we have to go back and face the real world with all its guilt trips. And we still have the big hurdle to jump." He gazed at her. "Maybe when it comes to that final moment, I won't be able to do it."

Her smile widened. "Oh, I think you will, judging from tonight."

He grinned back. "You could be right."

"So, when?"

"Tomorrow night? Oh, wait. Damn. I promised to fly my mom up to an antique show in Flagstaff tomorrow. Dad's going along, and he and I have appointments to look at some horses while we're up there."

She wrestled with her impatience. "How long will you be gone?"

"Three days. Until Sunday. Damn. I don't think there's any way I can get out of it, either. It's been set up for months."

"Three days sounds like an eternity."

"Tell me about it."

She traced the line of his jaw. "We could go back to my original plan and have you come back to my place tonight."

He gazed at her for a long moment and finally shook his head. "No. I really want this time to be one you'll remember."

"I don't think there's much doubt about that, no matter when it happens. And to tell the truth, I'm…afraid you'll change your mind in three days."

"After tonight? Are you kidding?"

"You had a good time tonight?"

He cupped her face in both hands. "I had the best time I've ever had in my life. And I promise you I won't change my mind."

Her heart swelled with an emotion she couldn't name, but it was strong, and it brought happy tears to her eyes. "Thank you, Mac. You're a true friend."

"I do my best."

"What time of day will you be home on Sunday?"

"Probably around noon."

"So you could come over that night."

"I could do that."

Her heart thudded in her chest. "Then I'll expect you about eight."

LEAVING TESS at her door that night was the toughest thing Mac had done in a long time. He hadn't told her, but he wouldn't have had to drive clear back to the ranch for birth control. He'd made it a practice to know where he could buy condoms on short notice, and there was a convenience store still open only five minutes from her house.

He was probably a fool for not taking her up on her suggestion and making love to her all night long. The thought of doing that made him ache. Now he had to wait three days for the chance. No matter that he'd been waiting all his life.

Wait a minute. *Waiting all his life?* Where had that come from? It couldn't be true. Surely Tess didn't have anything to do with his fruitless search for a wife. He just hadn't found the right woman yet. Oh, God. Maybe he had.

On impulse he swung into the Ore Cart Bar's parking lot and climbed out of the truck.

Suddenly a cold beer and a game of darts sounded like an excellent idea. He was still a young carefree bachelor. Bachelors were free to stop in for a beer whenever they wanted to, and he cherished that freedom.

Maybe tonight he sort of wished he could go back over to Tess's house instead of stopping for a beer, but that was only natural, considering how new the situation was. But the novelty would wear off with Tess, the way it had with all the rest.

That's what you think, taunted a voice that sounded a

lot like Tess when she was bound to prove herself right and him wrong. Over the years she'd infuriated him, made him laugh until he could barely stand, and worried him sick. But she'd never bored him. Mac walked into the bar, hoping a beer would silence that know-it-all voice that told him he'd started something that he had no idea how to finish.

The bar was fairly well deserted on this weeknight, but it had one patron that made Mac consider ducking back out the door. Unfortunately Dozer Blakely saw him before he got the chance.

"Hey, Big Mac!" he called from his bar stool. "Come on over and let me buy you a cold one."

Mac walked toward the row of stools and glanced around. "Where's Cindy?"

"At home." Dozer shoved a wayward lock of red hair off his forehead with a beefy hand. "Waitin' for me to cool off. Hey, Dutch, set the man up with his favorite brand, okay?"

"Will do," the bald bartender said. "How're you doing, Mac?"

"Can't complain." Mac sat down next to Dozer, but he would have liked to put more space between them. He could still smell Tess's perfume on his clothes, and he was afraid Dozer might recognize it. "Listen, should you be fighting with Cindy, her being P.G. and all?"

Dozer smiled. "When we fight, I'm the only one who gets upset. Cindy's cool as a cucumber." His blue eyes twinkled. "Hot date tonight?"

This would be tricky, Mac decided. "Why do you ask?"

"Oh, you look a little mussed up. I figured you might have been out parking."

"Could be."

Dozer smiled and took a sip of beer. "So, did you take that dunking last night to heart and decide to make up with Jenny?"

"Uh, no." Mac grabbed the beer Dutch scooted in front of him and took a big swallow.

"Babs?"

"Nope."

"Somebody new?"

"You could say that."

"But you're not talking, are you, Big Mac?"

Mac grabbed the opening. "No, Dozer, I'm not. I don't want you guys riding herd on me with this one, pestering me as to when we're going to tie the knot." He glanced at the hefty redhead and decided to go on the offensive. "And speaking of the knot, you're a sorry poster boy for the institution of marriage, sitting down here at the Ore Cart nursing a beer while your wife sits at home."

"I'm only doing what she told me." Dozer shook his head. "She's something else. I fly off the handle, just itching for a fight, and she won't fight. She tells me to go grab a beer and come back when I have something nice to say. In the meantime, she works on her cross-stitch, calm as you please."

"How do you know?"

"Because I usually sneak back and peek in the window to see if she's pacing the floor or banging things around, at least. You know, upset because I left the house. The hell of it is, she's not. So I come down here, drink my beer, and go home. She takes me back like nothing happened, and that's the end of that."

"What was the fight about? Or I should say, the fight she refused to have with you."

"Damned if I can remember." Dozer grinned sheepishly. "Knowing me, it was probably over something dumb. I tell you, I picked the right one when I hooked up with Cindy. Any other woman would have divorced me by now, with my short fuse. But Cindy knows it's just a passing thing, and she sends me off until I get over it. I love that woman something fierce."

"I'm glad for you." Mac picked up his glass again. "Here's to you and Cindy, and your diamond anniversary."

Dozer raised his glass in Mac's direction. "I'll drink to that." He took a long swallow, draining the glass before he set it down.

"Another beer, Dozer?" Dutch called.

"Nope. One's all I need, thanks." He turned to Mac. "Of course, if she ever threw me out for good, I'd drink the place dry."

"Sure."

"I've been meaning to tell you something, Mac."

"What's that?"

Dozer fished for his wallet and pulled out some money. "All kidding aside about Babs and Jenny, I can see why you didn't end up with them. They're both nice and all, and Jenny's built real sweet." He jiggled his cupped hands out in front of his chest. "Real sweet."

Mac didn't want to think about women's breasts, either. "And your point is?"

"You're a smart guy. You need somebody with brains. Babs and Jenny could never have kept up with you. You'd have been bored in a month or two."

"So I figured."

"Well, good. So, is this new girl smart?"

"Yeah, she's smart."

Dozer nodded. "Did you score yet?"

Mac winced. The type of evening he had planned for Tess didn't even begin to fit the definition of "scoring." He tried to imagine Dozer's response if he knew they were talking about his sister.

"Guess not," Dozer said, undisturbed by Mac's reaction. "Otherwise you would've grinned when I asked that." He laid his money on the counter and slapped Mac on the back. "Well, good luck with her, buddy. You deserve to find yourself a real nice lady. Maybe this is the one."

"Maybe." *Not.* As Dozer headed home to Cindy, Mac sipped his beer, determined to think of something else besides Tess lying alone in her bed. He even carried on a conversation with Dutch about the Arizona Cardinals' chances this year. When the beer glass was empty he added another bill to what Dozer had left and walked out into the warm night thinking how great it was to be a free man. He drove home with the windows down, a song on the radio...and Tess on his mind.

THE EVAPORATIVE COOLER had reduced the heat in Tess's little bungalow by the time she walked inside that night, but the place was still plenty warm. She closed the front door and with a sense of deep regret, listened to Mac's truck drive away. If only he still carried condoms in his wallet, then he could have stayed.

To make matters worse, he hadn't even kissed her goodbye. She understood why—nosy neighbors might have seen them and passed the word. She could spend all the time she wanted in Mac's company without arousing any suspicions, but one public minute in his arms would start every tongue in town wagging.

This particular business they had between them had to be kept private. She could still hardly believe he'd offered to take care of her problem himself. He was running a big risk that could potentially ruin his relationship with her brothers. And because she appreciated that so much, she intended to protect him as best she could. So she kept their goodbyes on the porch deliberately nonchalant.

But once she was inside the door and he was truly gone, she ran her hands over her breasts and closed her eyes, lost in remembering. Then she lifted her arms over her head and turned slowly in a circle, executing a subtle dance of celebration. By touching her and arousing her the way he had, Mac had given her a completely new sense of her body.

In the carefree days before puberty, she'd run and played with Mac and her brothers with no thought to the fact that she was a girl and they were boys. Then the changes had begun, and for the most part, she'd thought of them as a nuisance. As she developed, her body seemed to get in her way more than it helped her enjoy life. But now...now she understood what all those changes had been for. For *this*. Laughing in delight, she flung her arms out and whirled until she grew dizzy.

Feeling slightly drunk with the wonder of it all, she wandered into her bedroom, shedding her clothes as she went. She kicked off her sandals and padded barefoot into the bathroom, where she turned on the shower, adjusting the temperature until it mimicked the warmth of a lover's caress. She craved bodily sensation in a way she could never have admitted to anyone, least of all Mac.

She stepped under the spray, letting it beat down on

her. Then she flung back her head and lifted her breasts to the coursing water. Her nipples tightened and she touched them gently, reawakening the memory of Mac's loving.

Then she slid both hands down her water-slicked body to the juncture of her thighs, where she throbbed for him still. Her erotic books had been very clear—she didn't need Mac or any man to give her the kind of release she'd found tonight. She could take charge of her own pleasure.

And maybe someday she'd follow that advice, she thought, skimming her hands back up over her rib cage to cup her breasts once again. But tonight she wanted to savor the remembered sensation of his hands caressing her, coaxing her to enjoy the wonders of her body. Perhaps she was being silly, but it seemed to her that to work the miracle herself at this moment would dilute that precious memory.

She turned off the shower and toweled dry, paying careful attention to the task. Her body was no longer exclusively her domain, and the thought made her shiver with delight. She smoothed lotion over every inch of skin she could reach, taking her time, anointing herself as if she expected Mac to return.

He probably would not. He was, as she knew from years of experience, a man of his word. Once he'd decided that her initiation should proceed a certain way, he would follow through on that decision, ignoring his own needs, and even her arguments to the contrary. She wouldn't see him again until three days from now, at eight o'clock on the dot.

And perhaps he was right about this, she thought as she rubbed the scented lotion over her body. Perhaps there should be some ceremony and ritual to what they were about to do. She had three days to prepare. Three days to find tempting lingerie and turn her room into a lover's bower. Setting down the lotion, she returned to her bedroom and surveyed the situation. Most of it would have to change.

Grabbing a yellow legal pad and a pen from her desk drawer, she sprawled naked on her bed and began making a list.

8

THE NEXT AFTERNOON as Tess pulled packages from the car after her shopping trip to Phoenix, her neighbor, Hazel Nedbetter, came hurrying over with a florist's vase full of daisies. Tess quickly shoved the Naughty But Nice lingerie box under the front seat.

"I took these into my house so they wouldn't wilt on your front porch," Hazel said.

"Why, thank you, Hazel." Tess took the vase and stared at the cheerful bouquet of white and gold daisies, exactly like the ones on her dress. They could only have come from one person.

"It isn't even from the Copperville Flower Shoppe. The van was from some big florist in Phoenix. Can you imagine? The delivery fee must have been huge!"

"Probably was." At least Mac had taken some precautions, Tess thought. If he'd ordered from the local flower shop, the news would have spread by now. She was thrilled that he'd sent a bouquet, but she didn't know how in hell she'd explain it to Hazel. And Hazel would need an explanation. The more mysterious Tess was, the more Hazel would speculate and the wilder the gossip would become.

The sun beat down on them, and Tess needed to buy some time to think of what she'd say. "It must be three hundred degrees out here. Let's go into the shade," she said, starting toward her front porch. Doggone Mac, anyway. He'd put her in a precarious spot, but his reckless gesture made her smile. She could just hear him—*I wanted to send you flowers. I figured you're a smart girl. You'll think of something to tell the neighbors.*

Setting the vase on the porch rail, she turned to Hazel and used the first explanation she could think of. "I'll bet they're from my new principal in New York."

"Really? How fancy! I don't think Mr. Grimes ever sends flowers to the people he hires at Copperville High. They must do things differently back East." Hazel eyed the small white envelope secured in the arrangement with a plastic holder. Clearly she wanted Tess to take the envelope out and open it to prove that the flowers were indeed from Tess's new principal, as she'd speculated.

The envelope wasn't sealed shut, so Hazel could have looked at the card, but Tess didn't think she had. Still, it was possible, so Tess decided to go for broke.

She could pull this off, although Mac had given her quite a challenge. He knew good and well that the neighbors would notice flowers arriving at her doorstep and he was probably sitting in Flagstaff chuckling as he imagined her predicament. Even if she'd been home, the delivery van would have attracted attention. Most of her neighbors in this older section of Copperville were retired and had plenty of time to observe the activities surrounding them.

Determined to convince Hazel, Tess boldly plucked the envelope from the plastic holder. "Let's just see if I'm right." She opened the envelope, figuring whatever Mac had said, she'd tell Hazel it was indeed from her principal.

As it turned out, Mac had come to her aid. The cryptic card read *Wishing you the best as you explore new worlds—M.* Tess knew exactly what new worlds he was talking about, and they all involved the bed she was about to redecorate. But Hazel wouldn't realize that.

"Yep, it's from my principal, all right," Tess said. She repeated the greeting for Hazel and on impulse decided she could even nail her story down a little tighter. "My principal's name is Emma Kirkwood, but most people call her Em, or they use the initial *M* for short. See?" She turned the card around for Hazel's inspection. Tess had no idea if anyone called Emma Kirkwood *Em*, let alone abbreviated the nickname to an initial, but the chances of Emma appearing in Copperville were remote.

Hazel adjusted her bifocals and peered at the card. "Sure enough." She glanced at Tess. "That's real nice, sending you a bouquet like that. Although I would have thought maybe roses or carnations would be more likely than daisies."

"M likes daisies."

Hazel nodded. "Been shopping?"

With the change of topic, Tess knew she was home free. The daisies were explained. "Yes. Picked up some things for the trip." And it would be some trip, considering the supplies she'd found today. She thought Mac would be pleased. Maybe more than pleased. She wanted him to salivate, actually.

"When does Lionel plan on putting up a For Rent sign in front of your house?" Hazel asked.

"Not until next month, I think. Don't worry, Hazel. Lionel is very particular who he rents this place to. You'll get good neighbors."

"I suppose, but I'll miss you, anyway."

"I'll miss you, too, Hazel." Tess lifted the hair off the

back of her neck. Even the shade of her porch was darned warm, but if she invited Hazel in she might be there for another hour. She was a dear lady, and another time Tess might not have minded visiting with her, but at the moment she was eager to get her purchases inside before someone else showed up and noticed the lingerie box or the satin sheets.

"Your poor mother's going to cry her eyes out when you go."

"I know. I'll probably cry, too. But I have to spread my wings, Hazel. My brothers all got to be football heroes. This is a chance for me to shine."

"Oh, yes, your brothers. They might act like they don't care about such things, but they're going to hate having you so far away. And then there's Mac Mac-Dougal. That boy's going to miss you something terrible. I noticed you two were out last night. I was surprised at that, because Mabel Bellweather told me you were feeling sick when you were at the Nugget for dinner."

Tess began to wonder if she and Mac had any chance of keeping their secret, after all. Copperville was a hotbed of gossip. "I was feeling sick, but after I left the restaurant I started feeling better, so we took a long drive. He, um, wanted to discuss the breeding program he and his father are starting. They're going to look at a few studs during that big horse show in Flagstaff this weekend. You did know they're in Flagstaff?"

Hazel nodded. "I heard. Nora's at one of her antique shows up there."

"Right." Tess decided she needed to prepare Hazel for Mac's next move. "I made Mac promise to come over when he gets home and tell me all about the trip," she said. "So you'll likely see his truck here after they get home."

"Now, see there?" Hazel wagged her finger at Tess. "You two have always been close like that, sharing your news. Who's he going to tell about his goings-on when you're in New York City?"

Tess hadn't wanted to face that, herself. "I guess we'll have to use the phone. Well, Hazel, I'd better let you get to your dinner preparations."

"Guess so." Hazel seemed reluctant to take the hint. "How was Phoenix?"

"Hot," Tess said.

"I'll bet. These nights have been so warm I can barely sleep."

Which means Mac and I had better close the blinds good and tight, Tess thought. "I know what you mean," she said. "Well, see you later, Hazel. And thanks again for preserving my bouquet."

"You're welcome. Enjoy it." Hazel headed back over the path worn in the grass between the two houses.

Tess picked up the flowers and went inside. The phone rang the minute she set the vase on her coffee table. She walked over to the little telephone table next to the sofa and picked up the cordless receiver. "Hello?"

"Where have you been?" Mac asked. "I tried about six times today and kept getting your machine."

The sound of his voice made her nipples tighten. He'd never had that effect on her before, but times had changed. "I was in Phoenix."

"Oh, really? Buying more books?"

"Not this time. This trip was for other things." Her first impulse, because it was the way they'd always interacted, was to tell him everything she'd bought. But the dynamics had changed and secrets were very appealing now.

"Anything to do with...Sunday night?"

"As a matter of fact."

"What did you buy?"

She smiled. "Oh, something very, very brief."

"Really." The timbre of his voice changed. "Care to describe it?"

"I'd rather surprise you. Use your imagination."

"That's been my problem today. I can't seem to use anything but my imagination. I've been so spaced out my dad keeps asking if I overdosed on allergy medicine, even though he knows I don't have allergies."

"So you've been thinking about me." Her body reacted, moistening and throbbing as if he were right there beside her.

"That would be an understatement. I keep thinking about that daisy dress of yours, and...everything that happened last night."

"Me, too." She stroked the petals of her floral arrangement. "But the daisies were *very* hard to explain to Hazel Nedbetter, Mac."

His laugh was low and sexy. "I'll bet you came up with a story, though, didn't you?"

"I told her they were from my new principal, whose name is Emma, but she often goes by just the initial M."

He laughed again. "Damn, but you're clever. I wish I'd been there to hear you spin that yarn."

"Me, too."

His voice lowered, became soft and seductive. "I wish I could be there right now."

Tess sighed. "Me, too."

"What are you wearing?"

"A sleeveless blouse and shorts." Scenarios from her reading flashed through her mind, and she had the urge to experiment with her newfound power. "But it's very hot, Mac." She picked up the vase of flowers. "I think I'll just walk back into the bedroom and take my blouse off."

"*Now?*"

"Well, sure, unless you want me to hang up."

His tone was strained. "No, I don't want you to hang up. I might not get another chance to call you today. But Tess—"

"Just unfastening the buttons will help."

In her bedroom she set the vase down and started unbuttoning her blouse. "Ah. I can feel a little breeze from the air conditioner right here, blowing on my bare skin. By the way, did you find any good studs?"

"Uh, yes. No. Maybe. Have you got your blouse off yet?"

"I'm getting there. These buttons aren't the easiest in the world. I tell you, it's so warm here, Mac. This little trickle of sweat just rolled down between my breasts. I'll bet I'd taste really salty right now."

"You're..." He cleared his throat. "You're doing this on purpose."

"What? Taking off my blouse? You bet. Ah, there. That feels so much better." The joke might be on her. By teasing him, she was becoming incredibly aroused herself.

"What...color is your bra?"

"Ivory." Her breathing quickened. "Satin mostly, but the cups are a pretty lace. I like it because it hooks in the front, which makes it easier to take off."

His voice was low and dangerous. "Take it off now."

"You know, I think I will." She unfastened it with

trembling fingers and released her aching breasts. "It's…off. Oh, Mac, I wish you were here."

"Believe me, so do I."

"The daisies are so beautiful." She snapped one from its stem. "So soft." Slowly she drew the petals over her rigid nipples. "I'm stroking my breasts with one of your daisies, Mac."

He groaned.

"Little bits of yellow pollen are scattered over my breasts and nipples."

"God, Tess. How am I supposed to stand this?"

"You'll be here soon."

"Not soon enough."

She continued to administer the sweet torture of touching her breasts with the daisy. She pretended it was Mac's gentle fingers stroking her. "And if it helps, I'm aching right now, too."

"I hope so." His breathing rasped in her ear. "You deserve to be absolutely miserable."

"Are you?"

"Denim doesn't give real well, if that's what you mean."

"Too bad I'm not there to help you."

"Yeah, isn't it."

"I'm going to hang up now, Mac."

"I guess you'd better." His voice was tight with strain. "I'm at a public phone at the fairgrounds, and I'll have to stand here with the receiver to my ear and my back to the folks for a long time."

"Goodbye, Mac. Think of me."

"As if I have a choice. Goodbye, you devil woman."

She broke the connection between them and pressed the daisy against her breast. Sunday night seemed an eternity away.

MAC LISTENED to the soft click that ended the call, but he didn't put the receiver down. He hadn't been kidding about the bulge in his pants, and there was no way in hell he could turn around yet. He hadn't planned on the call turning into an erotic experience, not considering the thousands of times he'd talked to Tess on the phone. Mostly he'd been curious about how she'd handled the delivery of the daisies and if she was pleased with them.

I guess so, MacDougal, if she's rubbing them over that sweet body of hers. But he had to get that image out of his head or he'd never be able to leave this phone. Tess was amazing. When he'd suggested himself as her summer lover, he'd had no idea what a Pandora's box he was opening.

As he stood with the silent phone to his ear, he forced himself to think about something else. The exorbitant price that Stan Henderson wanted for his stallion, for example. And the fact that his father was seriously considering paying it. Finally he was able to hang up the receiver and turn around.

His father was standing not ten feet away, watching him.

"Hey, Dad." He walked over with what he hoped was a nonchalant smile. "I figured you'd be haggling with Henderson over that stud for the rest of the afternoon."

"I decided to take a break and let him think about my last offer." Andy MacDougal was a tall, lean cowboy who didn't look his age any more than Nora MacDougal looked hers. Most people assumed Mac's parents were younger, but they'd suffered through several miscarriages before he'd come along when Nora was almost past childbearing age.

"I'm guessing you've got girl trouble," Andy said. "Am I right?"

Mac grinned. A partial truth was probably his best approach. "You could say that."

"I also have a feeling she might be a serious girlfriend this time around."

Mac didn't like hearing that. "Nah. I'm not ready to settle down."

"Oh, I think you are. I've seen the way you look at the Blakely boys and their families. I also realize you're choosy, and that's fine. But I've never known you to be this distracted. So if the woman you've been trying to call all day long is ready for a home and family, then I suggest you go for it."

"She's not."

"Oh." Andy gazed at his son for a long moment. "Want to grab a hot dog and a beer and talk about it?"

"A hot dog and a beer sounds great, Dad, but there's really nothing to talk about."

Andy nodded. "If you say so. But the offer stands, anytime."

"I know that, Dad, and I appreciate it." Mac swung an arm over his father's shoulders. "Let's go eat. I'm starved."

THE OVERNIGHT MAIL TRUCK arrived in Tess's driveway the next morning. As she signed for the package, she noticed the Flagstaff postmark. Well, at least he hadn't sent another bouquet of flowers. She'd be hard-pressed to explain a second floral delivery from her new principal.

Once she'd bid the deliverywoman goodbye, she closed the front door and ripped open the package. Inside were a pair of unbelievably soft, furry gloves. She put them on and discovered they were too big for her, but inside one glove she encountered a folded slip of paper. She pulled it out.

Dear Tess,
I saw these in a clearance sale. I could have brought them with me Sunday night, but I decided I'd rather send them so you can spend the next thirty-six hours imagining how you will feel when I put them on and run my hands over every inch of your naked body. In the meantime, enjoy the daisies.

                                                        M.

With a cry of frustration she clutched the gloves to her chest. What an evil man. What a wonderful, delicious tease of a man. She smiled to herself. Just like when they were kids, they always had to get each other back. He'd sent the daisies and she'd tortured him over the phone. Now this. The score was definitely in his favor at this moment.

She put on one of the gloves and ran it experimentally over her bare arm. *Oh, Lord.*

"Knock, knock, can I come in?"

Tess leaped to her feet as her mother came through the unlocked front door, a habit she'd developed that Tess had seen no reason to change—until now. Heart pounding as if she'd been caught raiding the cookie jar when she was five, she shoved Mac's note in the pocket of her shorts and pasted on a welcoming smile. "Hey, Mom! How's it going?"

"I hadn't heard from you in a few days, so I thought I'd drop by and find out what you're up to. Darling, you look guilty as hell. What's going on?"

"Nothing, Mom."

Debbie Blakely raised her eyebrows, obviously not convinced. She was a small woman, and Tess had taken after her in height and hair color, although her mother's warm brown now came from a commercial product instead of nature. She was what Tess always thought people meant when they described someone as "pleasingly plump." Tess wouldn't have wanted her mother to lose an ounce, but she sure wished she'd be a little less perceptive.

Debbie glanced at the coffee table littered with the remnants of the overnight package and then at the gloves, one on Tess's hand and the other clutched against her chest. "What's that, a joke? Gloves in the middle of a heat wave?"

Tess thought fast. "That's what it is, all right. Mac sent them. It's his way of saying, 'Nanny, nanny, boo, boo, I'm in Flagstaff where it's cool and you're not.'"

Debbie Blakely laughed. "That would be Mac. And if I know you, you're planning your revenge even as we speak. Now I may have an idea what you're looking guilty about. Don't smuggle ants into his bed this time, Tess. It took Nora weeks to get them out of the ranch house."

"Right. No ants. Maybe I'll solder his boots to the horse trough, instead."

"Well, I promise not to tell. Want to do lunch?"

"Uh, sure." She'd planned to spend the day transforming her bedroom, but she could probably take time out for lunch.

"Good. I was thinking today that I won't be able to pop over here and invite you to lunch much longer, so I'd better take advantage of your being here while I can."

Tess walked over and gave her mother a hug. "I'll come home whenever I can. And I want you and Dad to visit me in New York whenever you can get away."

"Oh, we will, but…it won't be the same. My, those gloves are soft."

Tess had forgotten she was still wearing one. "Um, yes. I might actually use them in New York."

Debbie examined the glove. "Kind of big, aren't they?"

"Well, yeah, but it's the thought that counts."

"And no doubt Mac's thought was to torture you while he's enjoying the cool mountain air. He probably didn't care if they fit or not. Men."

"Scoundrels, all of them," Tess agreed.

"But we couldn't live without them, could we?"

"Guess not." Or so Tess was discovering. This was turning into the longest three days of her life.

"If you'll excuse me, I'll freshen up in your bathroom before we go," her mother said.

"Sure. Help yourself." Tess sent thanks heavenward that she'd decided to watch a movie last night instead of starting her renovations then. Satin sheets would have been a little difficult to explain to her mother, not to mention the angled mirror she planned to install.

"Oh, so these are the flowers you got from your principal," Debbie called out as she passed through Tess's bedroom into the bathroom. "Why don't you have them out on the coffee table?"

"I was enjoying them before I went to bed last night," Tess called back. Oh, my. Word traveled as fast as always around this place. She and Mac would have to have their wits about them. But they'd had a lot of practice being co-conspirators. Maybe she could think of this secret project as an extension of the pranks they'd pulled together over the years.

She looked down at the gloves. Then again, maybe not.

9

WITH SOME EFFORT Mac managed to smuggle a small cooler on board the Cessna Sunday morning without his parents noticing. Inside rested the bouquet of daisies he'd bought on the sly in Flagstaff and he'd used motel ice to keep them fresh in the cooler. Ice had never been an erotic substance to him until Tess had mentioned placing it against certain parts of his anatomy. Now he couldn't even look at an ice bucket without getting turned on.

And now, at long last, he was flying his parents back to Copperville. His rendezvous with Tess was only a few hours away, yet it was too many hours for his comfort. He hadn't dared call her again, considering the condition she'd put him in the one time he'd tried it. But she'd been on his mind constantly. He wondered what she'd thought of the gloves, and if she'd run them over her skin.

Picturing her doing that, his mouth went dry. Maybe she'd always been a sensuous person, but her reading had stoked up the fire in her. He wasn't going home to a timid virgin, that was for sure. But she was still a virgin, and no matter how she plotted to drive him insane, he had to remember to go slow and be gentle. That might not be as easy as he'd thought at first.

When he and his folks arrived home, Mac and his father unloaded the suitcases from the car while his mother went inside to check for messages on the answering machine. Mac walked into the kitchen in time to hear Tess's voice coming from the speaker.

This message is for Mac, she said, sounding like the Tess he'd known for twenty-three years, not the new Tess he'd just discovered. *Mac, don't bother to eat dinner before you come over tonight. I'll feed you. Something simple, finger food probably. Oh, and don't worry about ice. I have plenty. I might be out back or something when you get there, so just come look for me. See you tonight.*

Mac nearly dropped the suitcases he was carrying.

His mother turned to him with a smile. "You're seeing Tess tonight?"

"Yeah." Mac tried his best to look nonchalant, which wasn't easy while he was thinking about Tess feeding him some exotic food while dressed in whatever sexy outfit she'd bought. And then there was her subtle reference to ice, and the fact that she wanted him to walk in the unlocked door and come look for her. He'd bet a million dollars where he'd find her, and it wouldn't be "out back."

She'd cleverly created the whole message to sound normal, when it was filled with suggestive ideas that only he would understand. That was so like her. She'd done it to get him back for the gloves, no doubt. He cleared his throat. "I promised to drop by and let her know how the trip went," he added, realizing he was standing there staring into space. Not good.

Nora gazed at him, a speculative light in her blue eyes. "You're upset that she's leaving town, aren't you?"

"Not really. I'm happy for her. It's what she's always wanted."

"I know, and of course we're all happy for her, but

you're agitated about it. I could tell by the expression on your face just now. Your color was high. I think you're upset because she's going off and leaving you."

"I absolutely am not." Mac set down the suitcases, walked over and took his mother by the shoulders. "That imagination of yours is working overtime." Then he gave her a quick kiss on the cheek and noticed the tiredness around her eyes. Three days of being constantly on the go had taken its toll on both her and his father. He couldn't ignore the fact that they were both nearly seventy. "I think I'll ride out and check the stock tank Dad's worried about," he said.

"Wasn't he going to do that after we got unpacked?"

"Yeah, but why don't you two take the afternoon off? You both got a lot accomplished on this trip. Relax for the rest of the day."

His mother nodded. "I'll see if I can get him to do that. I think he's more worn out than he admits." She glanced at Mac with gratitude. "Thanks. I don't know what we'd do without you."

"Hey, no problem." Mac smiled at her and headed out the door. On the way, he passed his father coming in. "Try and get Mom to take it easy for the rest of the afternoon, will you? She's bushed."

"I need to check the stock tank."

"I'll do it. No point in both of us heading out there in this heat."

His father laid a hand on his shoulder. "Thanks. If I don't watch your mother, she'll run until she's exhausted."

"My thoughts exactly." Mac crossed the back porch and started toward the corrals with a sense of relief. The solo activity was just what he needed to get him through the next few hours.

WELCOME TO THE
CASINO!

Try your luck at the Roulette Wheel ...
Play a hand of Twenty-One!

How to play:

1. Play the Roulette and Twenty-One scratch-off games, as instructed on the opposite page, to see that you are eligible for FREE BOOKS and a FREE GIFT!

2. Send back the card and you'll receive TWO brand-new Harlequin Temptation® novels. These books have a cover price of $3.75 each in the U.S. and $4.25 each in Canada, but they are yours to keep absolutely free.

3. There's no catch. You're under no obligation to buy anything. We charge nothing — ZERO — for your first shipment. And you don't have to make any minimum number of purchases — not even one!

4. The fact is, thousands of readers enjoy receiving books by mail from the Harlequin Reader Service® before they're available in stores. They like the convenience of home delivery, and they love our discount prices!

5. We hope that after receiving your free books you'll want to remain a subscriber. But the choice is yours — to continue or cancel, any time at all!

So why not take us up on our invitation, with no risk of any kind. You'll be glad you did!

Play Twenty-One For This Exquisite Free Gift!

THIS SURPRISE
MYSTERY GIFT
WILL BE YOURS
FREE WHEN YOU PLAY
TWENTY-ONE

The Harlequin Reader Service® — Here's how it works:

Accepting your 2 free books and mystery gift places you under no obligation to buy anything. You may keep the books and gift and return the shipping statement marked "cancel." If you do not cancel, about a month later we'll send you 4 additional novels and bill you just $3.12 each in the U.S., or $3.57 each in Canada, plus 25¢ delivery per book and applicable taxes if any.* That's the complete price and — compared to the cover price of $3.75 in the U.S. and $4.25 in Canada — it's quite a bargain! You may cancel at any time, but if you choose to continue, every month we'll send you 4 more books, which you may either purchase at the discount price or return to us and cancel your subscription.

*Terms and prices subject to change without notice. Sales tax applicable in N.Y. Canadian residents will be charged applicable provincial taxes and GST.

If offer card is missing write to: Harlequin Reader Service, 3010 Walden Ave., P.O. Box 1867, Buffalo, NY 14240-9952

BUSINESS REPLY MAIL
FIRST-CLASS MAIL   PERMIT NO 717   BUFFALO NY

POSTAGE WILL BE PAID BY ADDRESSEE

HARLEQUIN READER SERVICE
3010 WALDEN AVE
PO BOX 1867
BUFFALO NY 14240-9952

NO POSTAGE
NECESSARY
IF MAILED
IN THE
UNITED STATES

HE'D NEVER BEEN so nervous and excited in his life as he drove toward Tess's house a little before eight. The sun was down and the streetlights on, but heat from the day still rose up from the pavement and he had the truck's air conditioner going full blast. Considering his heated condition, he might have to run the air conditioner in the dead of winter if he had a negligee-clad Tess waiting at the end of the line. Which wouldn't happen, because she'd be gone by winter.

The cooler beside him with a bottle of wine inside had been easy to pass by his parents. He'd taken wine over to Tess's house before. But he'd sneaked the daisy chain he'd made into the cooler when no one was around. His mother did seem to be watching him a little more closely, so he'd have to be careful about similar preparations in the future.

The future. A terrible thought came to him. Maybe tonight was all there would be. After all, once he'd taken care of Tess's virginity problem, she wouldn't need to continue this risky business, even though she'd be in Copperville for the rest of the summer. For some reason, he hadn't figured that out. He'd been "hired" for a specific job, and after tonight the job would be over.

Hell, he couldn't think about that or he'd be too depressed to enjoy himself. And he definitely planned to enjoy himself. If her brothers ever found out about any of this, his goose was not only cooked, it was fried, so he might as well make the reward worth the risk. Tonight would be one for the record books.

He parked in her driveway and discovered he was shaking like a newborn colt. The lights in the living room were muted, but he doubted that's where she was. Heart pounding, he got out of the truck with the cooler and walked up the steps to her front porch.

Sure enough, the front door was unlocked. He walked in, his chest tight from the effort to breathe normally, and stepped on a daisy. A trail of them led from the front door down the hall. He turned and locked the door.

Quietly setting the cooler and his hat on the coffee table, he opened the cooler and took out the daisy chain and the wine. First he glanced at the unopened bottle and then at the trail of daisies leading, no doubt, to her bed. If he didn't open the bottle now, it might never be opened.

Sidestepping the daisies, he walked into the kitchen, found the corkscrew and opened the wine. His hands weren't completely steady, but he managed to take two goblets from the cupboard without dropping them. With the daisy chain looped around one arm, the wine in one hand and the glasses in the other, he took a deep breath and started down the hall, following the daisies.

He'd prepared himself for the tempting sight of Tess lounging on her bed with very little on. After all, they'd gone swimming together hundreds of times, so he knew what she looked like in a bathing suit. This wouldn't be all that different, probably.

Wrong.

The scene she'd created left him breathless. His blood hammered through his veins as he gazed at every man's fantasy—a virgin trapped in a bordello.

Red velvet swags and red bulbs in the lamps gave the room a glow of sinful pleasure. His furry gloves lay waiting on a bedside table. On the other, a tray of food that could have been plucked right out of an orgy offered plump red tomatoes, velvet-ripe peaches, chilled asparagus, and clusters of moist grapes.

Whether it was the fruit or some exotic fragrance Tess had added, the room already seemed to smell of sex, and a stereo played soft, yet subtly persuasive music with an underlying beat that mimicked the rhythm of lovemaking. Gilt-framed mirrors propped at various angles all reflected the centerpiece of the room, a bed covered in virginal white satin and mounded with satin pillows of all shapes and sizes.

Reclining on that nest of pillows was a woman Mac barely recognized. Although the scraps of white satin covering her breasts seemed inconsequential, they managed to emphasize her cleavage, where the pearl necklace lay cradled by her soft body. His gaze traveled to the white lace garter belt and panties, which defined her femaleness in ways he'd never imagined. The garters were fastened to white silk stockings with a sheen like pearls and lace tops circling her thighs. Last of all he absorbed the fact that Tess, the woman who believed in no-nonsense running shoes and well-worn boots, was wearing a pair of white sandals with four-inch heels.

Tess gave him a slow smile. "What do you think?"

"I don't—" He swallowed. "I don't believe this is about thinking."

"True." Her gaze traveled to his crotch. "I have the reaction I wanted. Would you like…to get out of those clothes? They seem a bit…tight."

"Um, yeah." He looked down and realized he was still holding the wine bottle, glasses and daisy chain, but his brain was so fuzzy he couldn't decide what to do with them. It was a wonder he hadn't poured the wine on the carpet.

She held out both hands. "I'll hold the bottle. And

the daisies. I can pour us some wine if you want while you're taking off your clothes."

He gazed at her holding out her arms to him in that welcoming fashion and had the urge to toss the wine and glasses over his shoulder and join her immediately on that tempting bed. He groaned softly and shook his head to clear it. He'd need every ounce of control at his command in order to make this the slow seduction he'd planned.

"Is anything the matter?" she asked.

"Only that you've blown me away, and I'm struggling to get my bearings."

"I really did that?"

"Yeah, you really did that." He handed her the bottle and glasses. After she set them next to the tray of food, he gave her the daisy chain. "I'm usually a little more suave when I walk into a lady's bedroom with wine and flowers. I usually present them instead of waiting for her to ask."

"Oh." She grinned, and he caught a calming glimpse of the other Tess, the one who loved climbing trees and eating cotton candy. "Thank you for the wine and flowers," she said demurely. Then she put the daisies around her neck. They draped her breasts like a lei, drawing attention to the provocative swell above the tiny garment she wore. "How's that?"

"More exciting than I could have predicted."

She looked into his eyes, her own filled with an intensity to match his. "It is exciting, isn't it? Us, and...all of this. Who would have thought?"

"Not me."

She glanced at the wine. "The books say alcohol dulls sensual pleasure."

"I thought you'd need to relax." He chuckled.

"Maybe I need it more than you do. You don't look nervous at all."

"I have a million butterflies inside."

"You do?"

"Of course. I've never acted this way with a man in my life."

He was humbled as he thought what a gift she was giving him. "That makes tonight very special. For me, too."

"I'm glad. You know, maybe a little wine wouldn't hurt."

"I'm so keyed up I can guarantee it won't affect me."

"And I don't want to be inhibited."

He laughed. "This is inhibited?"

"Sort of. The books say that a woman can drive a man crazy if he comes into the bedroom and finds her...touching herself."

He gulped. "Really." From the painful bulge in his jeans, the books must be right. "And some wine might encourage you along those lines?"

"Maybe."

"Then drink up."

Her cheeks grew pink. "Just a little, then." She reached over to the nightstand and poured them each half a glass. Then she picked hers up and leaned back against the pillows. "Now undress for me, Mac. And make it slow."

His jaw slackened. "What do you mean, *slow*?"

"Tease me a little. Build the suspense." She swirled her wine in her goblet and took a sip, watching him over the rim of her glass.

His body quivered in anticipation while his mind balked. "What suspense? You've seen every part of me. And I can say that with conviction after the other night. What difference does it make how I take off my clothes now?"

"Believe me, it makes a difference. And keep your eyes on me the whole time you're doing it."

Suspicion made him frown. "How do you know it makes a difference?"

"A friend of mine in college had a male stripper for her twenty-first birthday party. He was very good."

"I'm not a male stripper!"

"Your body is even nicer than his." She rubbed the wineglass slowly back and forth across her lower lip. Then she circled the rim with her tongue and licked an imaginary drop off the side of the glass. She turned to him with a smile. "I'll make it worth your while, cowboy."

He wanted to laugh and make light of her blatant attempt to remind him of what she'd accomplished the other night. But the laughter stuck in his throat as he gazed helplessly at her mouth and remembered. With that gesture of her pink tongue moving over the wineglass, she probably could have persuaded him to drink arsenic.

He settled for drinking the wine she'd poured. Walking over to the nightstand, he picked up his glass and drained it. He set down the empty glass, took off his watch and laid it next to the glass. Then he emptied the condoms out of his pocket and put those on the table, too.

She glanced at them and back at him. "I have some, you know."

"How did you know what size?"

"I had a good idea."

He remembered her hands on him, her mouth taking

him in, and agreed silently that yes, she probably did know.

"So, will you strip for me, Mac?"

He gazed at her. "Swear to me you'll never tell anyone," he said as a last attempt at self-preservation.

"I swear on the tomb of old King Tut, take a willow switch to my butt."

That crazy rhyme they'd made up as kids took on erotic meaning when spoken by a sexy wench reclining in her red velvet and white satin room of seduction. "Is that a suggestion?"

"Not exactly. I haven't done much research into spanking fantasies." She picked up a remote control and pushed a button. The volume of the music increased a fraction, the beat becoming more insistent. "Now do it, MacDougal. Make me squirm."

TESS TRIED TO LOOK composed as she lay against the pillows and waited for Mac to undress, but inside she was churning with anticipation. He had no idea what a beautiful body he had, and in the past she hadn't allowed herself to admire it much, either. But that was then. This was now.

He'd worn a long-sleeved western shirt even though it was summer. Like most cowboys, he kept mostly long-sleeved shirts in his closet, because they'd protect his arms from whipping branches on a wild cross-country ride. If he got too hot, he'd roll the sleeves back, but Mac had come to her tonight in dress mode, the sleeves snapped at his wrists.

Slowly he unsnapped them, his habitual movements executed with tantalizing care. Her heartbeat quickened. He was really going to do this for her.

She sipped her wine as he started on the top fastener

of his shirt. Keeping his gaze on her, he made his way gradually down the row. Each soft pop of a snap was like the flare of a match lighting a new fuse. She hungered for each snap to release, each section of newly exposed skin.

He languidly pulled the shirt from his jeans so it hung open. She waited for him to take it off. Memories flashed by, more potent than she'd realized, of Mac stripping off his T-shirt and using it to mop his face when he'd helped her parents paint their house one summer, of Mac lying bare-chested beside the river one hot afternoon, his fishing pole anchored in the sand, his hat over his eyes.

She'd enjoyed the view then—she wanted it now. Instead, as if to gently torture her, he walked over to a chair and sat down. He drew off one boot with great deliberation, and then the other, all the while keeping his attention on her. His socks followed.

He's undressing because he's going to make love to me. The thought washed over her like a caress, moistening her with need.

He stood and walked toward her. "I've decided two can play this game."

"You have?" Her voice was breathy, not at all the way she normally sounded.

"You did a good job on the phone. If you unhook your bra for me now, I can watch."

She trembled. Darkness had protected her during their first encounter, distance and a telephone line the second. She wanted to be bold and daring this time, to experience the wonders she'd only read about. Mac was asking her to do that.

Following his lead, she drank the rest of her wine and set the empty glass on the table next to his.

"And do it slow," he murmured.

Heart pounding, she leaned back against the pillows and eased her fingers over the clasp holding the silken cups. Then she waited as he took off his shirt and she could finally admire his sculpted torso. With her eyes she traced the scar on his shoulder from a scrape with barbed wire, another on his arm from a run-in with a bull. The scars only made him seem more masculine.

He was magnificent. No wonder she'd loved wrestling with him when they were teenagers. She wanted to do more than that now.

He stood, hands on hips, and lifted his eyebrows, clearly indicating it was her turn.

She applied pressure to the clasp and it gave way, but she held it closed as she reached up and slid one shoulder strap down. Then she slid the other strap down. Slowly, slowly she allowed the garment to part and fall away, leaving only the pearl necklace and his daisies. The chain of flowers caught on one nipple, causing it to pucker. Instinct prompted her to brush the daisy chain across her other nipple, arousing it, too.

His gaze darkened and he sucked in a breath.

She paused and flicked her glance toward his belt.

His attention never left her breasts as he eased the buckle open and pulled the belt slowly from the loops. "Now touch them," he whispered.

Her heartbeat ratcheted up another notch. Sliding both hands up her rib cage, she cradled the weight of her breasts, lifting them as if in offering. Then she drew her thumbs down over the nipples, caressing herself.

"Oh, Tess." His hands shook as he unfastened his jeans.

The effect of sliding her thumbs over her breasts while he watched was incredible. Sensation poured downward to the juncture of her thighs, pooling and throbbing there, demanding satisfaction. Now she knew what fulfillment felt like, and she wanted it again.

He shoved jeans and boxers away, no longer measuring his movements.

The sight of his aroused body brought a quiet moan from her lips. Her desire had a shape now, as instinct made her aware of a hollowness that ached for what he could provide. More than release, she wanted to be filled.

He came to the edge of the bed. "You said you'd feed me."

"Yes." Her breathing was quick and shallow. "Whatever you want."

"That's good to hear." His voice was husky as he put a knee on the satin sheets. "I see what I want." He gently moved her hand aside and replaced it with his own.

At the remembered touch, her heart thundered in her chest. "Is there...anything I can do?"

"Arch your back," he murmured.

She did, lifting her breasts.

He used his teeth to lift the daisies away. When he drew her nipple into his mouth, she gasped with the realization that she was nearly at the point of climax. He'd had to coax her before, but no longer. Apparently this time she'd need only the fantasy they created in this room to become a wild woman. She hoped Mac was ready for that.

10

FOR THREE DAYS Mac had been dreaming about Tess's body. To taste and caress her breasts, to kiss and nibble and suck to his heart's content, was heaven. As the tempo of her breathing quickened, he lightened his touch, not wanting to bring her to the brink too fast. They had hours to enjoy each other. And besides, he knew where he wanted to be when she climaxed this time.

"You're so beautiful," he murmured.

"You, too." She ran her hands over his chest, brushing his nipples until they became as taut as the rest of him. She reached lower.

"Not yet." He drew back, knowing he couldn't tolerate her hands on him there until he was more in control. He teased the daisy chain over her skin, tinged rose by the lamps, and caused her to flush even pinker. Pollen scattered over her breasts and he licked it off. Then he took the pearl in his teeth.

Still fondling her breasts, he eased up and transferred the pearl to her mouth. As it lay against her tongue, he toyed with it with his own tongue in a blatantly suggestive way. He wondered if she knew that he was telling her, if she understood what he had in mind. If not, she would find out very soon. He was hungry for her.

With one last flick of his tongue over the pearl, he

lifted it from her mouth and eased downward, depositing it, moist and shining, in the valley between her breasts. "Do you know what I want now?" he whispered against her skin.

"I...think I do."

"Are you ready for that?"

Her breathing grew ragged. "If you are."

"I crave you. All of you."

Her breath caught. "But I...might go crazy."

"That was my plan." Heart racing, he began his journey, kissing his way along her downy soft skin to her navel. The scent of her cologne mixed with the perfume of crushed flowers and the heady aroma of arousal as he dipped his tongue into the small depression. She moaned and twitched beneath him.

He moved lower. The silk of her stockings and the ridiculously high heels excited him more than he wanted to admit, and he decided not to disturb any of it yet. The damp scrap of lace covering the object of his quest was easily drawn aside. Ah, she was so pretty. So drenched with need.

He touched her gently with one finger and she gasped. He kept his caress subtle as he planted lingering kisses along her inner thigh and ran his tongue over the lacy top of her stocking. Desire surged through him as he lavished the same attention on her other thigh, moving ever higher, ever closer to his goal.

At last he kissed her dark curls, and she moaned. When he finally touched his tongue to the delicate pearl nestled there waiting for him, she writhed beneath him. Suddenly impatient with the thin strip of lace denying him total access, he held it between his fingers and tore it with his teeth. Now.

Easing his shoulders under her silk-clad thighs, he

sought his reward. The taste of her made him groan with delight. As her cries of pleasure filled the room, he immersed himself in sensory overload, relishing the stockings, the shoes, the rosy light, the satin sheets, the erotic music, and most of all, the passionate woman coming apart in his arms.

Her climax came quickly, too quickly for him. She lifted her hips and he took all that she offered, but as she sank back, quivering and gasping, he settled in for a more leisurely exploration. She tried to wiggle from his grasp but she was weak in the aftermath of her release. He held her easily and continued along his chosen path. Before long her slight resistance faded and she opened to him in a wanton gesture that nearly brought him to the boiling point.

And he learned her—the touch that made her whimper, the stroke that pushed her closer, the teasing flick that drove her wild. As he coaxed her toward the precipice a second time, a fierce possessiveness took over. Rational thought played no part as he boldly claimed her, drawing from her the most intimate of sounds as she gave herself up to wave upon wave of shattering convulsions.

He brought her gently back to earth with feathery touches and light kisses over her thighs and dew-sprinkled curls. At last he drew slowly up beside her and brushed the hair back from her flushed face.

She gazed up at him, her gray eyes filled with dazed wonder. Her lips parted, but no sound came out.

He smiled. She looked the way he'd felt the other night. He was gratified that he'd created that sort of expression in her eyes. He trailed a finger down the curve of her throat and over her breastbone until he encountered the pearl on its golden chain. He brought it up slowly to his lips and kissed it before settling it back between her breasts.

Her gaze grew smoky and she ran her tongue over her lips.

He was glad to see a return of desire in those gray depths, for he was far from finished. And he loved knowing that the pearl necklace had become a symbol for the intimate activity they'd just shared. If he had it his way she'd wear it forever, and each time it moved against her skin she'd relive the sensations his tongue had given her.

"How do you feel?" he asked.

Her voice was low and throaty. "Like a concubine. How do you feel?"

"Like the luckiest man on earth."

She sighed. "That was way better than they described it in the books, and the books made it sound very nice."

He brushed his finger against her lower lip. "But you're still a virgin."

Her smile was pure seduction. "Feel free to take care of that anytime, cowboy. In case you can't tell, I'm putty in your hands."

His erection throbbed. She made the next step sound almost casual, and he tried to keep the same tone in his voice. "How about now?"

"Now's fine," she said lazily. She ran a fingertip down his shaft. "Unless you'd rather have me—"

"Not this time." He heard the edge in his voice. Damn, he was strung tight as a roped calf, and he figured there was only one way he'd be able to unwind. But in the process he didn't want her to absorb his agitation and tighten up herself. The whole point behind the way he'd just loved her was to ease her into this moment. Well, part of the point. In truth he hadn't been able to help himself. She was luscious.

"Do you want me to put the music on again?" she asked.

He became aware that the music had ended. He'd been so absorbed in her that he hadn't noticed. He thought about the music, considering. "Let's not," he said, combing his fingers through her hair. "I think this is a moment when we should listen only to each other, to anything we might say, to how we breathe…and the cries we make."

Her eyes darkened. "Okay."

He reached across her and took a packet from the bedside table.

"I could put that on for you. I've practiced."

"Practiced?" Jealousy hit him, swift and unyielding. "On who?"

"Mr. Cucumber."

He started laughing. "Only you, Tess."

"You think it's funny?" She grabbed the packet from him.

"Yes, I think it's hilarious." He give her a swift kiss and made a grab for the packet, but she held it out of reach. "Give it here." He kissed her again. This was sort of fun. Then he started chuckling all over again as he thought about her sitting in her kitchen studiously rolling a condom down a cucumber, over and over, until she got it right.

"I want to show you how good I am!" she protested, ripping the packet open.

"No." He made another grab but she evaded him. "Come on, Tess. I'm too worked up. If you fumble around you could set me off."

"I won't fumble."

"You will." He tackled her in earnest, laughing and kissing her everywhere he could reach as he tried to get the condom away from her. In the process he pulled off both her shoes so she wouldn't injure anything important.

"I'm good at this. Let me do it, Mac." She used the satin sheets to her advantage, wiggling away from him.

The wrestling match was putting him in even greater danger of exploding, but between sliding around on the sheets and coming into constant contact with Tess's bare skin, he was having a great, if risky, time of it. He'd always loved wrestling with Tess. "If you don't hold still and give me that condom, I'm going to tie you to the bedposts," he warned with a grin as he paused to catch his breath.

"I don't care." She was breathing as hard as he was. "The books say that's fun. Ever done it?"

"No." He looked down at her, his pulse racing at the vivid picture of her lying spread-eagle on the white bed, silken ties holding her wrists and ankles. He could barely breathe. "I was kidding," he said hoarsely.

"I wasn't. That seems like the perfect time for you to use the furry gloves."

He gazed into her eyes and saw the fire there. "You'd let me do that?"

Her chest heaved with her rapid breathing, making her breasts quiver. "I would let you do that, Mac, because I trust you. And you would let me do the same with you. It would be exciting."

"Oh, Tess." He began to tremble as a new picture formed—Tess tying him down and then…trying out all that she'd learned in her books.

"Lie down. Let me put the condom on."

"All right." She was messing with his head, making him want to surrender his role of leader again and let her tempt him into all sorts of new and fascinating sensuality. He lay back against the pillows. "But don't...play around."

"Don't worry. I understand your problem."

"I don't have a problem! Any guy in this situation would be struggling to keep it together."

"So you've had a good time so far?"

"You don't even have to ask. I—" He nearly choked as she leaned over him and took his erection into her mouth. "Tess!"

She lifted her head and smiled at him. "Lubrication." Then she expertly rolled the condom on in less time than he'd ever managed it and lifted her hands like a cowboy in a calf-roping event. "Done."

Despite her speed, the contact made him gasp and grit his teeth.

"Wasn't that pretty good?" she asked.

"Sure was."

"Want me to be on top? I've seen pictures of how—"

"No." He grabbed her and rolled, pinning her to the mattress. Then he reached for the garters and unfastened them. "And it's time to get rid of these."

She gazed up at him, her breath shallow and her lips parted in anticipation. "If you say so, macho man."

"Sometimes a guy has to take charge." He rolled each stocking down and pulled it off. Then he worked her out of the garter belt and what was left of the panties.

Her cheeks flushed as she lay there under his gaze. "Now do you approve? Am I ready?"

He was so overcome by the picture she made wearing only the daisy chain and the pearl necklace that he could barely speak. He lifted his gaze to hers and swallowed. "You're perfect," he said in a tight voice. He swallowed again. "And I should probably let you be on top and in control, since you've never done this, but I...don't want to."

Her question was breathy, seductive. "Why not?"

"Because I think I'd feel...secondary."

"Sort of...used?"

"Exactly."

"I wouldn't want that."

"Thank you." He stroked her breast, loving the softness beneath his palm as he cradled the supple weight and brought the nipple to a firm peak. "I'll be careful."

"I know you will." She closed her eyes and arched into his caress. "Oh, Mac, I could get addicted to having you touch me like that."

He paused, unsure how to respond. "We have all summer," he said at last.

Her eyes opened slowly, and excitement glowed in their gray depths. "Do we dare risk it? Making love like this all summer?"

He would risk just about anything to spend the summer loving Tess, but he didn't want to pressure her into anything she might regret. "That's up to you. It's your project. You said all you needed was deflowering."

"That was when I thought...it would be someone else. Mmm. That's good, Mac."

He rolled her other nipple gently between his thumb and forefinger. "The more we make love, the greater the chance someone will find out."

"Mmm. Yeah." She closed her eyes again and ran her tongue over her lips. "We should think about that."

"So think about it." He leaned down and drew one pert nipple into his mouth.

She sighed and lifted upward, encouraging him to take more. "Oh, sure. While you're driving me insane."

He tried his best to do exactly that, hollowing his cheeks as he drew her more fully into his mouth, letting her experience his hunger for several long seconds before he kissed his way to her other breast. "You don't have to decide now," he murmured against her skin as he slid a hand down to the damp triangle between her legs.

"That's...good." She drew in a quick breath as he tunneled his fingers through her curls and reconnected with her flash point. "And so is that."

Caressing her now took on a different meaning, because now, at last, he would know the wonder of being inside her. His blood sang in his veins as he stroked her, preparing her for that sweet invasion. And he would be the first. God help him, he was filled with joy at that thought.

TESS SENSED the change in Mac's touch, as if the promise of completion gave new urgency to every caress. And though she'd tried to seem casual about what was about to happen, in reality she felt like a canoe being carried down the rapids toward a thundering waterfall. If anyone but Mac had been touching her, arousing her, she would have leaped from the bed, unsure if she truly wanted this change in status, after all.

But Mac was there, making her ache, making her long for the firm thrust of him, deep inside her. Perhaps there would be pain. She no longer cared if only he'd finally claim her, complete her in ways she'd never dreamed of until this moment.

He lifted his head, a question in his eyes as he slipped his finger deep inside.

It was the penetration she longed for, but not nearly enough. A sudden shyness overtook her, causing her to close her eyes before she asked for what she wanted. "More," she whispered.

He eased two fingers in, placing soft kisses on her mouth. "Tell me how that feels."

"Different." Her breath caught as he moved his fingers gently back and forth. "Wonderful," she said, letting out a trembling sigh. "Mac, I'm going wild inside. Deflower me. Please."

His kiss was soft and lingering, but still she felt the barely leashed power of him as he moved between her thighs and propped his arms on either side of her head. Quivering with excitement, she wrapped both arms around his back and felt his muscles flex. She couldn't tell for sure because of her own trembling, but she thought he was shaking, too. His breathing was affected, at any rate, as he probed her gently with the blunt tip of his erection. She braced herself. No matter how much she might want him there, he would be substantial and might take some getting used to.

"Tess." There was a smile in his voice. "Open your eyes."

She gazed up at him, astonished by the tenderness in his blue gaze. She'd thought a man in his position would be in the grip of passion and appear much more fierce. "What?"

"You look just the way you used to before the roller coaster started. I'm going to go easy. You don't have to clench your jaw like that. And keep your eyes open. If you're looking at me, I'll be able to tell how I'm doing."

"How can you be so…calm?"

"Believe me, I'm not calm," he said quietly. "But I am paying attention."

"Oh, Mac. Thank you for being here."

"I'm here." He eased slowly forward and his eyes darkened. "Right here."

She noticed the flicker of uncontrolled desire in his eyes before she became totally absorbed by the sensation when he entered her. She registered warmth and size. He withdrew and eased in again, and she moaned in pleasure at the friction that was unlike anything he'd provided before.

"Tess?"

"That was a happy moan," she murmured, looking into his eyes. There was that flicker of primitive need again. She found it thrilling.

His breathing was labored, but he kept his movements slow. "I'm going a little deeper."

"Yes." Everything else, she began to realize, no matter how delicious, was only a lead-in to this, the ultimate connection. Nothing in her world had ever felt so right as opening her body to this man and being filled by him.

He slid forward, and met resistance. He stopped immediately and looked into her eyes. "This is it."

Her heart thudded wildly. One movement and her life would be forever changed. She would be a virgin no longer. Ah, but then she could welcome the whole length of him and know the wonder of joining intimately with another person. And not just any person, either. Mac. One movement and she could be fully with him, in every sense.

She slipped her hands down to his buttocks and gripped firmly. "Let's go for it."

As he pushed gently forward, she rose to meet him, determined to share in the moment. The sharp pain brought a cry to her lips.

"Damn." He stopped, his gaze troubled.

"It's okay." She trembled against him. "It's going away. Don't hold back. It's over now. Love me. Love me the way a man loves a woman."

With a groan he pushed deep, locking their bodies together, his hips cradled between hers. And the fierceness she'd expected to see earlier flared in the depths of his eyes as he gazed down at her.

As she met that gaze, she felt an answering intensity rise within her. She'd expected them both to be naked tonight, but she hadn't guessed he'd also strip her to the essence of her soul, and she him. She looked into his eyes and realized they were both seeing depths they'd never imagined before. And her world shifted, for she knew the connection they were making would not end with this night, or even with this summer. It would last forever.

11

PERFECT, Mac thought. He'd never been anywhere in the world that had felt so absolutely right as being here, as close as he'd ever been to Tess. It seemed as if their entire lives had been leading to this moment. Linked in spirit ever since they were children, they had finally created the ultimate link, and a sense of destiny washed over him.

Mindful of her tender condition, he moved carefully, but still he moved, needing to define and redefine that sword-to-sheath perfection they made together. "Okay?" he murmured.

"Very…okay." Her eyes shone.

He eased back and edged forward again. Yes. And again. *Oh, Tess.*

"Mac…Mac…"

The wonder in her eyes and the richness she poured into his name told him all he needed to know. She was with him. He cupped a hand beneath her bottom, steadying her as he transmitted a new, more urgent rhythm. She caught on quickly, rising to meet his thrusts. Her bottom was soft and yielding, sweet to hold, sweeter yet to knead gently with his fingers. Yet the flex of her muscles against his hand when she truly began to participate drove him wild.

Very wild. Soon. He changed the angle, brushing the tips of her breasts with his body, pressing against the sensitive nub between her thighs that would bring her with him.

Her breathing grew shallow and he knew he'd found the spot, if only he could last long enough. This first time, he wanted to give her the gift of knowing how good it could be, how much higher she could climb when he was deep within her, coaxing a response that would vibrate down to her toes.

Her eyes widened and her breathing quickened. He played to that response, urging her on. So good. He'd never dreamed making love could be like this. Her body rose to meet his thrusts, tightening around him. As the moment built in the depths of her eyes, exultant laughter bubbled from him.

"*Yes*," he cried.

"Oh, Mac!" She arched against him. "I'm—"

"Yes." His voice was hoarse with need. "You're a woman now." *My woman.* With one final thrust he brought heaven raining down upon them.

TESS SAT propped up against the pillows next to Mac, the tray balanced on another pillow across their laps while they sampled the snacks she'd prepared for the evening. Mac was eating with gusto, but Tess felt too happy and pleased with herself to be interested in food.

She looked at Mac for about the hundredth time, a grin on her face. "We did pretty good, huh?"

He lowered the peach he'd been about to bite into and gazed at her. A slow smile eased across his face, and he nodded. "Yep. You look damn pleased with yourself, too."

"*I am.*" She picked up a cluster of red grapes and plucked one off its stem with her teeth. "I'm proud of us. I think we were awesome. Better than I ever expected."

After swallowing his bite of peach, he gestured around the room. "I don't know. Looking at all this, I'd say you expected a lot."

"The books say a man is a visual animal, so I was trying to make sure you'd be properly aroused."

He laughed so hard he almost choked on his peach. "Overkill," he gasped. "Major overkill."

She lifted her chin. "I don't know how you can say that, considering how well everything worked out. Maybe if I'd left the bedroom the way it was, and worn an old T-shirt and boxers, you wouldn't have been able to get an erection."

He stared at her. "Tess, I had an erection driving over here just knowing what we planned to do tonight."

"Yeah?" She smiled. "So the phone thing worked?"

"I *knew* you did that on purpose!"

"Of course. Just like you sent the gloves on purpose."

"And you put that double-meaning message on the answering machine. I stood there listening to it with my mom watching me the whole time, if you don't think that was tough!"

"Well, I didn't want you to lose interest!"

"Fat chance of that, twinkle-toes."

"Seriously, Mac. According to what I've read, women are a lot better at sustaining lustful feelings in the absence of the lover than most guys. Guys are more the out-of-sight, out-of-mind type. I didn't want you to lose interest."

"For your information, there was no chance I'd lose interest. I didn't need that phone conversation or the message on the answering machine and your cute little reference to ice in order to get excited."

"Oh! I didn't remember the ice! I was planning to give you a special treat with that ice trick. But I was so carried away that I...forgot."

He gave her a long glance. "I'll take that as a compliment."

Her heart beat a little faster, remembering the glory of the moment when she'd felt completely united with him, as if their souls had fused. She'd lost all track of techniques and tricks in the wonder of loving Mac. "It is a compliment. I couldn't think of anything but what was happening between us." She held his gaze and heat invaded her secret places once again. "I guess we didn't need the ice."

"No. We didn't need anything but each other."

Even now, she could barely believe that he really and truly wanted her. "This is so new. Then you're really turned on by me, the girl you've known forever?"

"Uh-huh."

"Wow."

"In fact, I'm getting in the mood again."

And so was she, but she'd been hesitant to admit it. "I thought it took a while for men to recharge."

"It does. It's been a while."

"Not that long. From what the experts say, a man would probably need some stimulation before he could manage another episode."

Mac chuckled. "That reading may get you into trouble yet. Take my word for it, I could manage another episode. Maybe several. I wish I could stay here and make love to you all night, but I don't know how we'd ever explain my truck being parked outside your house all that time."

Tess glanced at the clock and sighed with regret. "You're right. The neighbors would wonder and the gossip mill would start running."

He nodded. "I could park outside somebody else's house all night with no problem, but not yours. And we sure don't want to awaken anybody's suspicions." He moved the pillow and the tray of food and swung his legs over the end of the bed.

Tess couldn't resist glancing at the part of his anatomy that had recently delivered her from her virgin status. "You *are* ready again!"

"Surprise, surprise." He reached for his clothes.

"Want a quickie?" Her blood raced at the thought.

He turned back to her, a smile on his face. "And what do you know about quickies?"

"Everything. You just forget about the foreplay and go for it." Her nipples tightened in reaction. "It makes for variety. What do you think?"

He paused, his boxers in one hand. "Sounds tempting. But I guess I need the answer to my question first."

"What question?"

He faced her. "Well, you're not a virgin anymore."

"No, I'm not."

"So your project's technically finished, right?"

Her stomach clenched with sudden anxiety. "You mean we could stop right here and never...make love again?"

"That's what I mean. I need to know if this is the end of the fun and games or not."

"What do you want to do?"

He gave her a wry grin and gestured toward his groin. "I think that's obvious."

"I'm talking about the long-term risk." But as she spoke, she wondered if she fully understood the long-term risk. She'd been concerned about their families and people in town finding out. Maybe that wasn't the biggest problem. After tonight she felt bonded to Mac in a way she'd never experienced before, and yet she'd have to break that bond at the end of the summer. The more they made love to each other, the stronger the bond would become.

"I'm willing to accept the long-term risk," Mac said quietly.

A world of meaning lived in that statement, she thought. "And we'll still be...friends?" She wondered if that was the most foolish risk of all. If they made love all summer, could they possibly continue to be just friends?

His reply was soft and deliberate. "We'll always be friends."

He looked magnificent standing there, she thought. No woman in her right mind would turn down the chance to spend the summer loving Mac, no matter what the consequences. "I wouldn't want to lose your friendship," she said.

"You won't."

"Promise?"

He smiled. "I swear on the tomb of old King Tut, take a willow switch to my butt."

She took a deep breath. "Then I guess..." She paused and blushed. "I guess I'd like to expand my summer project and get more...experience."

His smile faded, and he gazed at her with that unfamiliar fire in his eyes. "Okay. Then that's what we'll do." He started to put on his clothes.

"Wait. I thought we were going to have—"

"A quickie?" He pulled on his jeans and winced as he started buttoning his fly.

"Well, yes."

He reached for his shirt. "If tonight had been the end of the road, we would have. In fact, I might have turned it into something a little longer than that." He gazed at her as he buttoned his shirt. "But if we have all summer, then I don't want to settle for a quickie."

She wanted him so much she trembled, but she swallowed the words that would have begged him to stay. Still, she couldn't let him go without knowing when they'd make love again. Her hunger for his touch both startled her and warned her of the dangers ahead. "When are you...free again?" she asked. No matter how hard she tried, the neediness in her voice seeped through.

He crossed to the bed and sat down. Leaning toward her, his shirt half fastened, he cupped her face in one hand. "Are you going to get all prissy and try to pretend you don't want me so much you can't see straight?"

Of course he could read her like a book. She should have realized that. "I—"

"Because that's how much I want you. I'm practically blinded by how much I need you, how much I want to be inside you again. I don't want to leave tonight, but we both know I have to, and the sooner I go, the easier it'll be for both of us." His thumb brushed her lower lip. "I want to see you again tomorrow night, and the night after that, and the night after that. Hell, I want to spend all summer here in your bedroom."

"You do?"

"I can't think of anything sweeter. But we have to watch it or we'll make people suspicious. We need to wait a while before we get together again."

She moaned in frustration.

"That's better. At least you're being honest about what you want."

She gazed into his eyes, helpless in the grip of passion. "I didn't realize making love would be so...so good."

"It isn't always."

"I figured that, from the cautionary tone of the books. The first time is supposed to be pretty awkward because the couple isn't used to each other."

He caressed her cheek. "That's where we have the advantage. We already know how the other one thinks."

"Maybe not completely. You see, I was afraid that familiarity would make me boring for you."

"Oh?" His eyebrows raised. "Why? Am I boring for you?"

"No, but I've never done this before. You have."

"But not with you."

"So having sex with me is not boring?"

He smiled. "Not by a long shot."

"Good." She smiled back. "Then how about we do it again Tuesday night?"

He shook his head. "Too soon. And Wednesday's poker night. That should be quite a test, come to think of it."

"Mac, you're torturing me."

"No more than I'm torturing myself. Listen, Thursday night's a full moon. Let's take a ride to the river."

Her pulse rate skyrocketed. "Am I supposed to wear a dress with nothing on underneath?"

He grinned. "Good memory."

"As if I could ever forget that dream of yours!"

"Well, I won't ask you to do that. You'd be uncomfortable, and your hair's too short for that particular fantasy, anyway."

"I could wear a wig."

His smile widened as he combed his fingers through her hair. "I like your hair the way it is. But you might wear as little as possible without making a big deal of it. And don't worry about being thrown to the ground. I'll bring a blanket. And a couple of towels."

"Towels?"

"Ever gone skinny-dipping?"

"Of course not. My brothers would have had a fit if they thought I was swimming nude in the river." She gazed at him. "Have you?"

"A time or two."

"With a girl?"

"Maybe."

She was insanely jealous, but she didn't want him to know. She glanced away. "It's naive of me to think you wouldn't have. Did you take them…down to our hide-away?"

He guided her chin around until she had to look at him again. "Do you honestly think I would take someone else to our spot? To go skinny-dipping and…other stuff?"

She hoped he wouldn't, but she'd never asked him not to. "It's a good spot."

"It's *our* spot. I wouldn't feel right taking someone else there. I'm insulted that you could even think such a thing."

"Oh, Mac." She couldn't help the happy smile she gave him. "I would have so hated you taking someone else there, even if you didn't go skinny-dipping or have sex with her."

"I know. That's why I'd never do that. But I want to

make love to you there, on the sand. And maybe even in the water."

Her body moistened, imagining exactly that. "I don't know if I can wait until Thursday night."

"Me, neither. But we don't want to ruin everything. In the meantime..." He leaned closer and kissed her, his tongue taking firm possession of her mouth.

She grew hot and dizzy from the suggestive movement of his lips and tongue and the memory of all the pleasure he'd given her. By the time he drew back, she was struggling for breath.

"Come to the corral about seven-thirty Thursday night," he murmured.

"I will." She tried to pull him back for another kiss, but he left the bed.

His voice was hoarse. "I really have to go, or we'll be tumbling around on that bed all night and we'll both be in trouble." He finished dressing. "I'll see you Thursday night."

It seemed like an eternity, but she knew he was right. People were used to them doing things together, but not constantly. "Okay. Thursday night it is."

He started out of the room and turned back. "I suppose you'll have to change the room, in case anybody shows up."

"I probably should. But I could put it back again sometime if you'd like."

"Oh, I'd like. We have some unfinished business in this room—something to do with silk ties and furry gloves."

She was going wild inside. "Mac, if you drove your truck down to the bar, and walked back, maybe we could—"

"No." He gripped the door frame as if to keep himself from walking back into the room. "Leaving is best. I don't want anybody reporting my truck was at the bar all night, either. And there's always the chance I'd be seen leaving your house in the early-morning hours." He glanced at her. "If we really want this secret to keep all summer, then we have to be careful not to blow our cover."

She sighed. "I guess you're right."

"Aren't I always?" He gave her a cocky grin.

"No, you are not, you arrogant man!" She laughed and threw a pillow at him.

He caught it in one hand. "Your aim's off, Blakely. You must be out of practice. When was the last time you threw a baseball?"

"I don't know. Want to practice Thursday night instead?"

"Not on your life."

"Then get out of here. I have more reading to do."

The comment had the desired effect, making the flame leap again in his eyes. "You really know how to get to a guy."

"I promise to tell you all about what I've read when we get together Thursday night."

"Want to bring a flashlight and a book along? We could glance over it together."

"Sure, why not? Sort of like reading comics together in the tent after dark."

He laughed. "Not even close. Oh, and by the way, congratulations on your new status."

"Thank you. I think I'm going to like it."

"I know I am. This is by far the best summer-project idea you've ever had." With a wink, he walked down the hall.

Tess listened until she heard the front door close.

Then she got up and threw on a robe before walking down the hall. Maybe he'd change his mind and come back in, needing to hold her again as much as she needed to hold him.

Unfortunately he really seemed to be leaving. After he slammed the truck door shut, the engine roared to life and the headlights flicked on. She automatically walked over and flashed the front-porch light, their goodbye signal. He flashed the headlights of his truck in return. Then he backed the truck down the driveway.

She could hardly stand to have him go. He'd taken her from innocence to knowledge, and now she craved him with an intensity bordering on obsession. Maybe she would have felt this way about any man who had introduced her to the wonders of physical love, but she doubted it.

For one thing, not any man would have known her well enough to make this such a mind-bending experience for her. Not any man would have had the tenderness and caring Mac had demonstrated every step of the way. And she couldn't imagine any other man looking so beautiful in the act of love.

As she stood in the living room listening to the fading sound of his truck's engine, she discovered the fatal flaw of her great plan. If she couldn't bear to have him leave after one night of lovemaking, what condition would she be in when the summer came to an end?

12

TESS WAS LOOKING for any distraction to get her through until Thursday night. When Hammer's wife, Deena, called Tuesday morning to suggest a day at the community pool with whichever Blakely women and kids could make it, Tess jumped at the chance.

Deena, a freckle-faced brunette who had been one of Tess's best friends in high school, was a teacher's aide. She had summers off, which was a schedule she intended to keep until five-year-old Jason and four-year-old Kimberly were older. Joan brought Sarah and Joe, and Cindy found somebody to work her shift at the auto-parts store so she could ease her pregnant self into the cool water. Only the newlywed Suzie, a bank teller, couldn't get off.

"And wouldn't you know, she's the one who looks the best in a bathing suit," Deena said as the group of women staked out a corner of the fenced pool area with lawn chairs, beach towels and a cooler containing sandwiches and juice.

"Oh, I don't know that Suzie wins the bathing-suit competition," Joan said. Like everyone else, she'd worn her suit under her T-shirt and shorts and was now stripping off her outer layer. "Tess is looking pretty buff in that red tank suit."

Tess glanced down at herself, suddenly self-conscious. "Hey, it's the same old me."

"Maybe so," Deena said. She grabbed Jason and swiped some sunscreen lotion on him. "But you're looking real good, chick. Been working out or something?"

"Nope." She hoped she wasn't blushing. Surely the fact that she was no longer a virgin didn't show somehow. Inside she felt like a changed woman, but outside she must look exactly the same. Mac wasn't that much of a miracle worker.

"They're right," Cindy chimed in. "There's a certain glow about you." She laughed. "People say pregnant women get that, and I'm still waiting. Mostly I just feel fat."

"I think you're all seeing things." Tess felt desperate to get out of the spotlight. "Come on, kids! Who's ready to go for a swim with Aunt Tess?"

A chorus of *me, me, me* followed immediately.

Tess had helped teach all of them to swim, and consequently they were all fish, even four-year-old Kimberly. Tess gazed down at their eager faces and felt a pang of regret. They would grow so fast while she was gone. She must remember to cherish days like today, and not count them as time-fillers until she could see Mac again. "Last one in's a rotten egg!" she called, and leaped into the pool.

Three hours later the women gathered their tired group together, put more sunscreen on pink noses and decided the perfect ending to the day would be treats all around at the Creamy Cone. Tess pulled on her shorts and sandals, ran her fingers through her hair and decided not to bother with the T-shirt. In the summertime, shorts worn over a bathing suit became almost a uniform for patrons at the Creamy Cone.

Everyone piled into Joan's minivan for the four-block trip, and on the way Tess sat in the back with the kids and led them through "The Itsy Bitsy Spider" and "I'm a Little Teapot."

"Carry me, Aunt Tess," Kimberly begged when they arrived at the bustling ice-cream shop.

"Too many cannonballs into the pool for you," Tess said, hoisting the little girl out of her seat and propping her on her hip.

"I *like* cannonballs," Kimberly said, snuggling against Tess.

"Yeah, you sprayed me all the time," added her brother, Jason.

Tess laughed. "Me, too. This girl's a regular spray machine."

"Hey, look!" shouted Joe, Joan's six-year-old. "Uncle Mac's here!"

Uncle Mac. Of course the kids had always called him that, considering that he was an honorary Blakely, but today, after she'd been hearing herself referred to as Aunt Tess for hours, the title struck her differently. Aunt Tess and Uncle Mac.

The idea hit her with more force than any cannonball jump of Kimberly's. Uh-oh. She hadn't subconsciously been having *that* little fantasy, had she? If so, she could forget it right now. Mac was only helping her out. Sure, he might be having a good time in the bargain, but if he'd ever considered having a relationship with her, he would have spoken up long before this.

And he certainly could have spoken up on Sunday night, she thought as she watched him get out of his truck. Instead, he'd been more intent than she was on keeping their secret. Nope, he definitely didn't have dreams of happily-ever-after with her.

"Hey, Uncle Mac!" Joan's daughter, Sarah, called. She started to run across the parking lot.

"Sarah!" Joan yelled a warning and bolted after her as a low-slung car pulled quickly into the lot, apparently oblivious to the running girl. Sarah had a good head start on her mother.

Still holding Kimberly, Tess ran forward, too, knowing neither she nor Joan would make it in time.

At the last minute, when Tess was too horrified even to scream, Mac hurtled into the path of the car, snatched Sarah out of the way and leaped to safety.

The driver, a teenage boy, slammed on the brakes and jumped out of the car. "Oh, God! I didn't see her!" he wailed. "Is she okay?"

Mac held a quaking Sarah tight in his arms. He was breathing hard. "I think so." He leaned away from the child. "You okay, sweetheart?"

Her voice was muffled against his shirt. "I...think so."

"Sarah!" Joan reached them and wrapped her arm around the girl's shoulders. "Did you get bumped? Does anything hurt?"

"N-no." Sarah sounded close to tears.

Joan sagged with relief as Cindy and Deena came up and put comforting arms around her. Everyone started talking at once, exclaiming over the close call, while Joan took several deep breaths and the color seeped back into her face.

Finally Joan held up her hand for silence. "Put her down, please, Mac. She and I are going over to that tree and having a little talk about running in parking lots."

"I don't run," Joe announced.

"Me, neither," said Jason.

"Me, neither," piped up Kimberly from her perch in Tess's arms.

"And we're going to hold you all to that," Mac said, glancing at each of them with a stern expression.

The teenager stepped toward Joan. "I'm sorry, Mrs. Blakely. I shouldn't have driven in so fast. I just got the car today, and I was all like, wow, I want to show my friends. But if anything bad had happened to her…"

Joan took Sarah's hand and gave the teenager a weary smile. "Fortunately it didn't. It's Eddie, isn't it?"

"Yes, ma'am. Eddie Dunnett."

"Well, we're lucky, Eddie. Hopefully we've learned something without suffering a tragedy in the process. Sarah shouldn't have been running without looking, and you should probably remember how dangerous parking lots can be around here, especially this one in the summer."

"Yes, ma'am." Eddie glanced at Mac. "Thanks, Mr. MacDougal. Thanks a lot."

"I'm glad I still have some reflexes left," Mac said.

"Yeah, no quarterback at CHS could run the option play like you. My dad still talks about it."

Mac looked uncomfortable. "That was a long time ago. So, is everybody ready for some ice cream? I'll treat."

"In that case, I'll have the jumbo banana split," Deena said with a grin. "I was going to settle for a small cone, but if the gentleman's buying—"

"Okay, but I'm gonna tell Hammer you took advantage of me," Mac retorted.

Deena laughed. "You're lucky he's not here. He'd order the Earthquake."

"If he was here, I wouldn't have offered to treat.

Come on, everybody. Let's see what kind of bill you can run up."

"Sarah and I will be in shortly," Joan said. "Joe, you go with the rest of them so I can talk privately with Sarah."

"Come along, Joe," said Cindy, holding out her hand.

Tess had always liked the way members of the family accepted responsibility for all the children, not just their own. A Blakely grandchild had a host of adult role models, and from where Tess sat, they were all good ones. Then if you added Uncle Mac, a true hero, a kid would have no excuse for not turning out well.

As for Sarah, she looked completely miserable for ruining the mood of the day. For a sensitive little girl, that was punishment enough. "Come on, gang," Tess said, adjusting Kimberly on her hip. "I'm in the mood for vanilla dipped in butterscotch."

"That's my favorite," said Mac, falling in beside her. He reached over and tugged gently on Kimberly's blond curls. "How's Kimmy today?"

"Uncle Mac! You're messing up my hair!"

"It's already messed up! You've been doing cannonballs in the pool, haven't you?"

Kimberly laughed. "Yep."

Tess wondered if Mac realized that in reaching over to tease Kimberly his arm had brushed Tess's breast. But if Mac didn't realize it, Tess did. All at once she became aware of her own unkempt hair, her pink nose and her wrinkled shorts. Until a few days ago, she'd never thought about what she looked like when Mac was around. Now she wished she'd at least taken time to comb her hair.

"We all got a little messed up today," she said.

"That's okay." He reached over and tweaked Kimberly's nose, getting a squeal in response. "I like my girls messed up."

This time she was sure he was aware that he'd brushed against her. The movement might have seemed accidental to someone else, but Tess felt the deliberate nature of it. He held the door of the shop open for her, and as she walked by him, she registered the heady scent of a slightly sweaty, thoroughly masculine Mac. He wore a T-shirt and jeans today and looked sexier than any man had a right to. She fought her reaction to him, knowing that she couldn't let any of her feelings show in front of her sisters-in-law.

"So you can take a break any old time and sashay into town for ice cream?" she asked, glancing at him. Oh, but he looked good, with his hat tilted at a rakish angle and a gleam in his eye. "Must be a cushy job you have, MacDougal."

"Not as cushy as yours," he said. "Frolicking in the water with this bunch all day while I'm out there busting my butt repairing fence."

Kimberly leaned over Tess's shoulder to peer behind Mac. Then she giggled. "Your butt's not busted, Uncle Mac."

That's for sure, Tess thought, remembering the muscled firmness she'd gripped when they'd…whoops. Dangerous territory. Thoughts like that would make her blush, and blushing wasn't something she normally did when Mac showed up. She stepped into line at the counter behind Cindy and Joe. Mac stood behind her, and she could feel his presence as clearly as if he'd pressed his body up against hers.

Kimberly peered over Tess's shoulder at Mac. "When I grow up, I'm gonna marry you."

"That makes me one lucky guy," Mac said.

Tess shivered, remembering those words in a far different context than playful banter with a little girl.

"Unless I marry Buddy in my Sunday school instead," Kimberly added solemnly. "He's always trying to kiss me."

Tess jiggled her and spoke with mock sternness. "Hey, you little heartbreaker. You can't propose to one guy and then announce you're marrying somebody else the next minute. You have to make up your mind."

"Okay. Then I choose Uncle Mac."

"Thanks, Kimmy. Can *I* give you a kiss?"

"Oh, sure. Just don't slobber like Buddy."

"I'll try not to." Mac leaned forward and kissed her on the cheek. "There, it's official."

They were all just kidding around, Tess told herself. There was no reason for this tightness in her chest, no reason for her to feel suddenly grief-stricken at the thought that Mac would have a real engagement one of these days. No doubt he'd even ask Tess to be in the wedding. After all, they were best friends.

Her turn came to order, and she got a butterscotch-dipped cone for herself and a chocolate-dipped one for Kimberly.

"That's all?" Mac said as she stepped aside so he could order. "No triple banana split or Earthquake for either of you?"

"I like chocolate-dipped the best. I always get that," Kimberly said with authority.

"Tess? You're going to let me get away with just a butterscotch cone?"

"Yep." She set Kimberly down and handed her the chocolate cone before taking the freshly dipped butterscotch one from the counter clerk, a young woman named Evie Jenkins. "Thanks, Evie."

As Kimberly walked over to the table where the rest of the group had gathered, Tess turned back to Mac, who looked more tempting than any ice-cream cone. She realized that her sisters-in-law were engrossed in eating their ice cream and keeping their children from becoming sticky disaster areas. They wouldn't pay any attention to her and Mac, especially considering they were used to seeing the two of them tease and joke with each other.

A devil took temporary possession of her, and she gave Mac a sultry glance. "As much as I'd like to take advantage of you, this is my all-time favorite." Then she swirled her tongue around the top of the cone.

Mac stared at her.

"Then if you nip off the top—" she bit through the butterscotch coating "—you can suck the ice cream right out." As she demonstrated her technique, she glanced up at Mac.

He continued to stare at her while gripping the counter so hard his knuckles showed white against his tan.

"Mr. MacDougal? Are you ready to order?" asked Evie.

Mac didn't take his gaze from Tess. "Uh, yeah." His voice was gravelly. "I'll have...what she's having."

"Coming up."

"I can't believe you're doing that," he murmured to Tess.

"Eating ice cream?" She smiled innocently. "That's what everyone does at the Creamy Cone."

"Not like that."

"Exactly like that. I've eaten one of these like this a million times."

"But not after we've just…"

She took a quick inventory of the area below his belt and was gratified with the slight bulge there. "I can't imagine what you're talking about."

"Oh yes you can," he said in a low voice. "Imagination is your long suit. You love to torture me, don't you?"

"What's good for the gander is good for the goose. You were playing games with me as we walked in here, while you were pretending to fool with Kimberly."

"That was only—"

"Mr. MacDougal? Here's your cone. Oh, and the other ladies said you were paying for everyone."

"That's right." It seemed to take great effort for him to turn away from Tess and focus on the task of paying the bill.

Tess moved a little closer. "I'll see you over at the table," she said softly. "And thanks for the dipped cone."

He slipped his wallet back in his pocket. "If I'd known what you were going to do with it, I never would have agreed to buy you one," he muttered without turning around.

"Fair is fair." Feeling much better than she had when she'd been mired in thoughts of his eventual marriage, Tess walked over to join the others.

MAC PLAYED abysmal poker the following night, and the Blakely brothers finally figured out that a woman must be distracting him. Although they teased him about being lovesick and pestered him for the name of his latest conquest, he managed to outmaneuver their questions. By the end of the evening no one was the wiser.

His latest conquest. He chuckled at the irony of that as he stuffed a blanket and two beach towels in his saddlebags Thursday night in preparation for his ride with Tess. Tess had conquered *him*, more like it. He was afraid to put a name to what he was feeling in relationship to Tess, but he craved her nearly every waking minute, and that wasn't a good sign. He'd thought tonight would never get here.

No other woman had ever made him come unglued so fast. Maybe it was all the reading she'd done, or maybe she was a natural when it came to exciting a man. In any event, her instincts would do justice to some Hollywood sex kitten, and yet she had no real experience with men other than him. Oh, how he loved knowing that. He loved it way too much, considering that the status quo would change. More men lived in New York City than in all of Arizona. She had a damn good chance of finding at least one who was to her liking.

He pushed that notion out of his head, not wanting to ruin the night. And it was one hell of a beautiful night. The moon sat just below the mountains, creating a glow that threw the familiar ridge into stark silhouette. Any minute now the moon would poke its head over, looking huge and golden as it crested. Mac hoped Tess would get here before that happened, so she could see it with him.

He'd always liked sharing stuff like that with her because she was so passionate about the beauty around her. He should have known that she'd transfer that passion to anything she did, especially making love.

Passion and curiosity—it was quite a combination. He wondered if she'd remember to bring any of her books.

The sound of her car pulling in beside the barn made his pulse rate go up. She rounded the barn just as a sliver of the moon eased up over the ridge.

"Come over here and see the moon," he said.

She quickened her steps. "I hoped I'd get here in time." She reached his side and leaned her forearms against the top rail of the corral as she watched the sky. "Oh, wow."

He leaned casually against the rail next to her, his arm barely brushing her arm, as if to prove to himself he could be alone with her and not grab her, as if he were in no hurry to leave and go down to the river. As if he didn't want her with every fiber of his being.

When she'd hurried toward him, he'd figured out from the lovely jiggle under her T-shirt that she wasn't wearing a bra. If he had to make a guess, he'd say she'd skipped the panties under her shorts, too. She held a book and a small flashlight in one hand. All of that made a potent combination, and he was more than ready to forget about the moon.

But he'd promised her they would always be friends, and Tess was the sort of person who remembered promises like that. She'd expect that someday they'd be able to stand here and watch the moon rise as friends, the way they'd done many times before. He might as well start practicing now.

But the air was filled with her scent, and his heart raced as he thought of holding her soft body again. He hungered for the taste of her lips, although he wouldn't dare kiss her here. Either one of his parents could come out and catch them.

"How was poker?" she asked.

"I lost every hand."

"Mac!" She turned toward him. "That's not like you. In fact, you usually come out ahead of everyone else."

"Your brothers were extremely happy about it. They wanted the name of the girl I was seeing, so they could thank her. They figured that was the only thing that would make me completely hopeless at cards."

"But it wasn't really me that was the problem, right? It was having to face my brothers after having sex with me."

"I guess so." Although he wasn't quite sure about that. He'd suffered some guilt pangs for the first half hour or so of the poker game, but after that, the guilt had seemed to wear off. From then on he'd lost because he was daydreaming about Tess, but revealing that might give away more than he wanted to right now.

"So what did you tell them?"

"Nothing. I just let them speculate."

"Do you think they'll try to find out who you're seeing?"

"Oh, they'll ask around, but I don't think anyone will think of you. As I've said before, no one would ever suspect what's going on between the two of us. We could probably kiss in the middle of the park in front of the whole town, and they'd think it was brotherly and sisterly affection going on."

"Do you feel like kissing me now?"

He stared at the moon. "Yeah, I do."

"More than kissing?"

His groin tightened. "Yep."

"I just wondered. You seem so cool and collected. Weren't you the one who told me not to get all prissy and pretend I didn't want you so much I couldn't see straight?"

He looked at her and saw a beautiful face silvered by moonlight, sparkling eyes that drew him like a moth to flame, moist lips that made him crazy to taste her again. "I want you so much I can't see straight."

"Then what are we doing standing here gaping at the moon?"

"Beats the hell out of me." He pushed away from the fence. "Let's go."

13

BEING ON A HORSE in his current condition wasn't the smartest move he'd ever made, Mac realized as they went down the trail, but riding to the river was the only option. Walking would take too long, so he had to make a compromise between speed and comfort.

The moon lit their path and gave him an arousing view of Tess moving along ahead of him, her hips swaying gently in rhythm with Peppermint Patty's brisk little walk. When the trail curved so he caught her in profile, he became more convinced that she didn't have a bra on under her shirt.

And then she took off the shirt.

He could hardly believe she was doing it and wondered if he was having another potent dream, complete with crickets chirping and an owl hooting in the distance.

A few moments later the shirt came sailing back toward him, and he was so dumbfounded he was barely able to snag it before it dropped to the ground. "Hey!"

"What?" She turned in the saddle, giving him a breathtaking view of her breast bathed in moonlight.

"What are you doing?"

Even from this distance, the mischief was obvious in her smile. "Getting you hot."

"I'm already hot!" Squirming in the saddle, to be

more accurate. Panting, lusting, longing for relief from this agonizing need to be deep inside her.

"Then hotter."

"Damn, Tess." Her shirt was scented with her cologne, and something even more erotic, the fragrance of Tess, aroused and ready for love. He bunched it in one fist and held it to his nose. Oh, Lord. That scent…memories of lying between her thighs, of tasting her, whirled through his fevered brain. "Why does your shirt smell so…good?"

"A little trick I read in the book I brought along tonight."

"What trick?"

"Oh, you just find a way to convey your own…special perfume to your lover. They say it works better than any manufactured perfume from the store."

He watched her through a haze of desire. "They would be right. You're not wearing panties under your shorts, are you?"

"No."

"So you took this shirt and put it—"

"In a very special place. Then I sent it back to you. You know, the motion of this horse is…*very* nice."

Mac groaned. "Ease up on me, Tess. I'm a desperate man."

"The book says anticipation is everything."

"Bull. Anticipation is excruciating." He heard the gurgle of the river ahead. Almost there. Smelling the water, the horses picked up the pace, and he tortured himself with imagining the sweet jiggle of Tess's breasts in the moonlight. He reached down and pulled the blanket out of his saddlebag and tucked her shirt in its place. He had no intention of wasting time once they got to the river.

Tess headed Peppermint Patty down the embankment and was off her horse in no time. She left the mare ground-tied, as she and Mac always did when they came down here at night. The horses weren't going far in the dark, and they provided a good warning system for snakes.

Mac's view of Tess was blocked by her horse as he dismounted holding the blanket. But when she stepped out from behind Peppermint Patty into a pool of moonlight, Mac lost his grip on the blanket. She was naked.

"Does this come close enough to your fantasy?" she murmured.

As he gazed at her standing in the silvery light like some nymph from a fairy tale, the water rippling and flashing behind her, his throat tightened with desire. "It goes beyond it," he said huskily. "I don't think I could dream something this beautiful, so I sure hope you're real."

"I'm real." She walked toward him across the sand and he noticed the small book in her hand. "And I want to make love with you, Mac."

Make love. His throat ached with emotion as he faced the truth—making love was exactly what he'd be doing, perhaps for the first time in his life. But for Tess, this might only be a stepping stone, an initiation into pleasures she would one day enjoy with another man. He had to protect his heart. "I see you have your reference book, there," he said, trying to keep his tone light.

"You said you wanted to see it."

"Oh, I do." But technique didn't seem to matter so

much now. Still, she wanted an education, and he'd been chosen to help her learn. That in itself was an amazing gift he'd been given, and to expect more would be greedy. He leaned down, picked up the blanket and shook it out, settling it on the sand. She stretched out on it while he started taking off his clothes with shaking hands.

The process took longer than he wanted because he couldn't stop looking at her lying there like some sort of nature goddess. He never would have guessed that their old meeting spot by the river could turn into such a seductive place. More than seductive. Tess made his heart ache with her beauty.

Sunday night she'd totally captivated him with her white satin and rose-colored bedroom, but there was something even wilder about this scene. Not far away a pack of coyotes howled and yipped, hunting, perhaps even mating by the light of the full moon. The sound stirred basic instincts deep within him. He'd do well to ignore them. They could only get him into more trouble.

"Coyotes," Tess said.

"Yeah." He took off the last of his clothes and reached in the pocket of his jeans.

"They sound so…primitive."

He caught the note of urgency in her voice, as if her reaction was the same as his. Heart pounding, he knelt beside her on the blanket. They were only playing at this, he told himself. He would be crazy to get serious. "So, professor, what do you want to try?"

She opened the book and leaned away so that moonlight fell across the page. "This."

The coyotes howled again as he gazed down at a black-and-white artist's drawing of a couple mating in the way that wild creatures mated. He sucked in a breath, knowing that was what had filled his mind as he'd listened to the coyotes' song, yet never imagining she would want such a thing, too. But oh, to love her like that, with the night sounds around them and the river rushing by…he ached with the wanting of it.

He glanced at her and a tremor passed through him. This primitive mating would have great significance for him, which made it dangerous, but for her it might simply be a unique experience. "You're…sure?"

Slowly she closed the book. Then she sensuously rolled to her stomach. Before he realized it, she'd risen to her hands and knees, offering her round bottom in the age-old invitation of a female to her chosen male.

His body could not refuse. Hot blood thrummed through his veins as uncivilized needs took hold of him. Grasping her hips, he moved into position behind her. A guttural, untamed sound rose from his throat and he fought the urge to drive deep and claim her in the way of the wilderness. Instead, he probed gently, not wanting to frighten her.

Desire surged in him when he found her moist and ready. Still he held back, slipping his hand around her waist and down, massaging the tight nub that heightened her response. With a little cry that was almost a plea, she tilted her hips, and he could restrain himself no more. He slid smoothly into her waiting channel.

And for the second time in his life he felt an incredible sense of connection, even stronger than the first time. And with that arose an urge he'd never known— the compulsion to pour himself into this woman and watch her grow round with child, his child. His body chafed against the barrier he'd placed between seed and womb and called for him to complete the connection and fill her with his essence.

And he could not. With a groan of pleasure mixed with deep frustration, he drew back and pushed forward with more force, lightly slapping her with his thighs. She murmured encouragement, and he increased the pace, pummeling her gently yet firmly as the sandy clearing filled with the sounds and scents of mating. They became slick with sweat in the heat of the night air as the slap of flesh against flesh grew faster and more defined. Their gasps and soft cries melded with the call of night creatures, the wind in the trees and the ripple of water over stones.

She tightened around him a moment before she was rocked with convulsions. Her undulations drew him into more frenzied movements as instinct told him now was the time, the time to plant his seed. He erupted in a forceful climax, crying out her name and holding her close to receive him. And the mating dance that had shaken him to his soul came to a powerful...and fruitless...end.

TESS LAY on the blanket, curled with her back nestled against the protective curve of Mac's body, and wondered how she'd created such a terrible problem. She'd fallen madly, passionately, desperately in love with her best friend. What had started out as fun and games, a fine adventure together before she headed off to her new life, had become more important than anything else in her world.

She didn't believe a woman should sacrifice a bright future in order to be with a man. Yet that's exactly what she wanted to do. She knew that Mac wouldn't leave Copperville as long as his parents needed him on the ranch, so any woman who wanted to be with Mac would have to stay in Copperville, too. And she wanted to be with Mac, to make love with him, to laugh and play with him and make babies with him.

Especially make babies. She wanted to be his mate, to make love again the way they had a little while ago, only without protection. She'd leaped from being a virgin only days ago to wanting it all—marriage, motherhood, years of lovemaking with this man.

It wasn't the way she'd pictured herself. From as long as she could remember, she'd been determined to escape the confines of this small town, to be sophisticated and worldly. She'd vowed to live in a big city, travel to exotic places, have many lovers.

Then, when she'd tired of all that, she'd settle down, probably right here in Copperville, and raise a family.

Now all her worldly plans seemed hollow and lonely. What good was any of it, if she couldn't have Mac there to share it with her? She'd rather stay here and be a ranch wife than lose Mac.

Not that Mac was asking. He'd never given any indication that he thought of her in those terms. He didn't act as if he wanted to settle down and marry anyone, as a matter of fact, let alone her. He'd never even been engaged.

He stroked her hip. "Whatcha thinking about, twinkle-toes?"

She decided on a partial answer. "Oh, just that it's too bad I'll be heading for New York the end of August."

He kneaded her thigh. "Because this is so much fun, you mean?"

"Yes." More than fun. She'd become involved, heart and soul, but she dared not tell him.

"It's fun, but in a way it's a good thing we have a limit on the time we can be together. We'd never be able to keep it a secret if it went beyond August."

"True." Perhaps he was happy with the secret arrangement, considering that he wanted to keep his status with her brothers intact. The only way her brothers would tolerate a sexual relationship between Mac and Tess was if they were getting married. Immediately. Mac didn't want marriage at the moment, apparently, so the secret had to be kept.

"Ready for a little skinny-dipping?"

She turned toward him. "We're really going to?"

He gave her a quick kiss. "Sure. We're all hot and sticky. It'll feel good. And besides, it's part of your education."

"Mac, I don't think we can have sex in the middle of that river."

"Why not?" His grin flashed in the moonlight. "Because it isn't in your book?"

"Because you won't have a pocket to stash your condom in."

"Tsk, tsk. You take away a girl's virginity, and suddenly she thinks sex is only about intercourse." He got to his feet and pulled her up with him. "Come on. Let's see what happens when you stand thigh-deep in rushing water without a bathing suit on." He took her hand and led her toward the riverbank.

Excitement swelled within her. That was another thing she loved about Mac. He had a heck of an imagination. Still, she wondered if he'd thought of that sort of stimulation on his own. "Have you been reading my books?"

"Nah. But I went down to the drugstore and bought one of those magazines they keep behind the counter.

The article was about hot-tub jets, which we don't have, so we'll have to improvise."

And improvise he did, although there was much laughing and splashing and playful groping before he finally had her positioned the way he wanted her. He'd so awakened her sensuality that he easily convinced her to accept the river as a teasing lover. Holding her steady, adding his own caress to that of the water, he coaxed her to let the current stroke her intimately, bringing her to a crescendo of feeling. At the moment of release she couldn't tell whether the bubbling water or Mac's caress had sent her over the edge.

While she was still gasping in reaction, he swept her into his arms and carried her back to the blanket. He made love to her while they were both still wet and slick as otters, so their bodies slid together as if they were oiled. She'd never known such triumphant freedom. She felt lithe and supple, capable of anything. They twisted and turned on the blanket, exploring different positions, alternate ways their bodies could move and shift yet still give unbelievable pleasure.

She was sure Mac was enjoying himself. His murmured words told her so, and when his tone roughened, she knew he was in the grip of fierce passion. When at last he surrendered to that passion, she held him tight and absorbed the strong tremors that shook him. She couldn't imagine living without this, without him. Perhaps, if she loved him well enough and thoroughly enough this summer, he'd realize he couldn't live without her, either.

THE SUMMER PASSED far too quickly for Tess. For every creative lovemaking scheme she dreamed up, Mac came up with one to match it. She suggested a day trip to Phoenix. They checked into the honeymoon suite of a hotel where no one would know them and spent the day in bed. He flew them up to Flagstaff where they hiked to a mountain meadow and made love in a field of daisies under a bright summer sky.

They experimented with velvet ropes, furry mittens and feather dusters. While they were in Phoenix they stopped into an X-rated boutique and dared each other to buy something. They came out of the shop with body paint and flavored massage oils.

The charged hours Tess spent with Mac seemed painted in brilliant color, while the rest of her life seemed to be cast in shades of gray. She went through the motions of a normal summer, playing cards with her sisters-in-law every Wednesday night, baby-sitting for her nieces and nephews, having lunch with her mother, planning the surprise anniversary party for her parents. But none of it seemed quite real, because she couldn't tell those she cared about that a most significant and wonderful thing had happened to her—she was completely in love with Mac MacDougal.

And she wanted to tell the world. She especially longed to confide in her mother, who would be a great source of advice. When her sisters-in-law discussed their husbands, whether in frustration or delight, Tess wanted to be a part of that conversation, to join the ranks of women openly, proudly in love.

Mac seemed just as involved with her as she was with him, although not a word of commitment ever came from his mouth. During the hot weeks of summer, they shared everything, it seemed, except a future. It was as if she were about to be shipped off to war and might never come back, so the subject of a happy-ever-after could never be broached.

Aside from that, she thought they were no different from any other couple just discovering passion and love, except that their relationship was known only to themselves. At first she'd thought secrecy was essential to her summer project. Sharing the secret with Mac had felt delicious and naughty. Now she was sick of it. But she couldn't tell. Not ever, unless Mac agreed, and she couldn't imagine him agreeing. And that made her soul ache.

By THE FIRST WEEK in August, Mac had come to the painful conclusion that he should break up with Tess. He should have ended their affair long before this, in fact. He was obviously good enough for her in bed, but not good enough to consider altering her career plans for, not good enough to let the world know about their love affair. He'd watched for any wavering on her decision to move to New York, and there was none.

As he headed to her house for another night of lovemaking, the truck splashing through puddles left by a heavy afternoon rain, he cursed himself for being weak. If he couldn't treat sex with her as a casual roll in the hay, fun while it lasted but forgotten when it was over, then he should get out now and start putting himself back together.

In fact, that's what he'd do, by God. Tonight. He wouldn't make love to her. He ignored the sick feeling of disappointment in his gut at that thought and vowed to carry through with what was right, what would ultimately save his sanity.

He'd walk into her house and tell her this activity was eating into his time, causing him to get behind on some paperwork for the ranch. That much was true. He'd taken over the books for his parents a couple of years ago, and at the moment he was making a sorry job of it.

He arrived at the town's traffic light as it turned red, and although his was the only vehicle at the intersection, he stopped anyway. As he sat waiting for the green, a horn beeped behind him.

Glancing in the rearview mirror, he spotted Rhino Blakely's truck with Rhino driving and Hammer in the passenger seat. Mac raised a hand in greeting and fought down the guilt that swept over him every time he unexpectedly met members of Tess's family. Tonight he didn't have to feel guilty, though. He was going over to Tess's house, but he wouldn't be there long. It was over.

Rhino hopped out of the truck and ran forward to knock on Mac's window.

Mac rolled it down. "What's up?"

"Joan and Deena went to a movie, and me and Hammer feel like a darts tournament at the Ore Cart tonight. What do you say?"

Mac hesitated only a split second. If he had somewhere to go, that would force him to make the break with Tess. "Sure. I have to swing by Tess's house for a few minutes, but I can be there in a half hour or so."

"Great. Light's green." Rhino ran back to his truck.

Mac rolled up the window and crossed the intersection. Fate must have stepped in to make him take this necessary step, he thought. Here he'd been thinking of what he needed to do, and along came some help in the form of Rhino and Hammer. If he ended it with Tess tonight, the brothers would never find out about the wild activities going on under their noses.

Even Tess probably needed some time to regroup before she went to New York. She might not realize it, but she'd probably have a tough time giving up what they'd shared this summer.

The rest of the way to Tess's house, Mac ran through all the reasons to end the affair. They were all good reasons, yet he felt as if someone had dropped a load of copper ore on his chest as he walked up the steps to her porch and opened the door. Walking away from another night of wonderful lovemaking and knowing he wouldn't make love to Tess ever again might be the hardest job he'd ever given himself. He'd have to be strong.

14

EXOTIC MUSIC with a pulsing beat drifted from Tess's bedroom, and automatically Mac became aroused just wondering what she had in store for him. Whatever it was, he'd resist.

Not that resisting would be easy. With each rendezvous they planned, he always wondered what she'd come up with that would surprise the hell out of him. And totally turn him on. He and Tess had tried stunts that had never crossed his mind with any other woman.

Yet now that he thought about it, sexual adventure suited Tess perfectly. She'd tempted him with bold ideas when they were kids, too. The raft they'd built and almost drowned trying to ride, the wild-horse roundup, the cave-exploration trip—Tess had thought of every one of those.

God, it wouldn't be easy walking back out of here tonight and giving up the excitement of loving Tess, the pure fun of just being with her. But that was short-term thinking. For the long term he needed to start learning to do without Tess's soft mouth, her warm, moist body, her... He stood in the doorway and felt his resolve slip away.

Tess was dancing. And not just ordinary dancing, either. She wore filmy pants that hugged her hips, a jeweled bra dripping with gold coins, a gold armband and a veil across her nose and mouth. She was a vision straight out of a sheik's harem, complete with tiny cymbals attached to her fingers. She kept time with them as she rotated her hips in the most mesmerizing rhythm he'd ever seen.

"Surprise." Her grin was faintly visible behind the veil. "I've been practicing for weeks." She continued to dance as she motioned him to a straight-backed chair in the corner of the room. She'd obviously placed it there for her audience of one. "And now I'm going to dance for you and drive you insane. Enjoy."

The light veil had the most incredible effect, emphasizing the sultry look in her eyes and making him hungry for her mouth simply because he couldn't see it very well. By covering her lips, she made them seem more exciting and forbidden, more of a prize when they were finally claimed.

Not that he would be claiming them. He had something to say, and that would eliminate the chance of kissing those temptingly disguised lips of hers.

But he couldn't make his announcement immediately. After all, she'd been practicing this dance for weeks to surprise him. He ought to at least let her show him what she could do. Courtesy demanded it.

Besides, he couldn't seem to take his eyes off the circular motion of her hips. He wondered what that would feel like if…no. He wasn't going to make love to her tonight, so it didn't matter what that would feel like. Fantastic, probably. But he was ending it. Definitely. Once she'd finished her dance.

He slouched in the chair and tried to look slightly bored as she danced slowly around him. When the beat became faster, so did the motion of her hips. He swallowed. Then she began adding a new dimension, a gentle shimmy of her breasts that made the dangling coins dance. He licked his dry lips.

She drew closer, brushing his arm with her hip as she danced. Her shimmy increased in speed, and she leaned forward, shaking her breasts so close to his face he could see the tiny drops of perspiration in her cleavage. The pearl necklace rested there, as it had all summer. And looking at it never failed to get a response from him.

"Unfasten your jeans," she whispered.

He glanced quickly into her eyes. This wasn't going at all the way he'd thought it out. "No, Tess, I—"

"Do it," she whispered more urgently, dancing around him, her hips keeping that maddening, erotic rhythm. "I want you now, Mac. And I can tell you want me."

"But—"

"Now." Still dancing, she took off the finger cymbals and reached beneath the snug band around her hips for a small package she'd obviously hidden there earlier. She swayed closer, her arms undulating with the music, and tucked a condom in his shirt pocket.

He was lost. If he didn't go along with her plan, she would be very disappointed. She had this scene all worked out and had gone to a lot of trouble to make it happen. Besides, he was so aroused he was in pain. He couldn't walk out of this room now if his life depended on it. He worked clumsily at the buttons of his fly, his heart pounding as he focused on the fascinating shimmy of her breasts and the amazing rotation of her hips.

He took the condom out of his shirt pocket. Then he nearly dropped it when she reached between her legs and somehow made the crotch of the filmy harem pants come undone without missing a beat.

"Are you impressed?" she asked softly.

"Oooh, yeah." And shaking with need. He managed to get the condom on as she danced closer, the coins jingling from the quivering rhythm of her breasts.

"Hold perfectly still," she whispered. "I'm going to do it all."

Incredible as her body looked as it moved, he was completely captured by her eyes. Emphasized by the veil, her eyes seemed to smolder with more fire than ever before. He couldn't look away.

Still keeping time to the music with her hips, she braced both hands on his shoulders and straddled the chair. Then she slowly lowered herself in a sensuous, rotating movement that made him gasp with pleasure. Yet he wouldn't, couldn't close his eyes. As she used all the sensuous dance movements to make unbelievable love to him, he focused on the blazing heat in her eyes, searching for the depth of emotion that rocked him whenever they came together like this.

And he found it. As her rhythm increased, her eyes told him that yes, she felt what he felt, that her heart had been branded as surely as his.

"I love you," he said. For the first time in his life the words meant something special, something so real he could almost touch it.

Her eyes were pure flame. "I love you," she murmured.

Joy surged so intensely through him that at last he closed his eyes, afraid she'd see his tears of relief. She loved him. Everything would be okay. As her movements grew more uninhibited and her cry of release filled the room, he held her tight and abandoned himself to a soul-satisfying climax.

They stayed locked together for many long minutes, Tess's veiled cheek resting on Mac's shoulder. He gently stroked her back, unsure what to say next. He really wanted the first words to come from her—something along the lines of *I've decided not to go to New York. I love you and I want to stay here with you.*

They'd honeymoon in New York, he decided. They'd take lots of trips, in fact, to make up for the loss of her big adventure. They'd—

"Yo, Big Mac! Where are you, buddy?" The unmistakable sound of Rhino's voice came from the direction of the living room.

Tess scrambled from Mac's lap and ran to the bedroom door. She slammed it and plastered herself across the door frame, her eyes wide.

"Oh, God." Mac stared at her. He'd completely forgotten he'd promised to meet Rhino and Hammer at the Ore Cart, and that he'd told them where he was headed in the meantime.

"Hey, Mac!" Rhino called again, this time obviously from the hallway. "What's going on?"

Mac swung into action, jumping from the chair. "We'll... I'll be out in a minute!" he called. "Lock that," he muttered to Tess.

"Why can't you come out now?" Rhino sounded suspicious.

"Just give me a minute, okay?" When he heard the lock click Mac headed for Tess's bathroom.

"What's going on in there, Mac?" Rhino's tone had changed from suspicious to angry. "Is Tess with you?"

"Yes, I'm with him, Rhino. Go on out to the living room. We'll be there soon."

Mac finished quickly in the bathroom. "God, I'm sorry, Tess," he said as he returned, buttoning his fly on the way.

"It's not your fault." She'd taken off her jeweled bra. Topless, she pulled a plain one out of a drawer.

"Yes, it is my fault. I met them when I was driving over here. I told them I was on my way to your house but I'd meet them in a half hour for darts."

She turned in the act of fastening the front clasp of her bra. "Why would you—" She paused. "You weren't planning to stay, were you?"

"No."

Her face grew pale. "You were going to end it, weren't you?"

"Well, yes, I was, but I—"

"Never mind the long explanation." Her voice quivered and she turned away from him. "Just get out there and talk to them while I get dressed."

"Tess, dammit, I—"

"Go! I mean it, Mac!"

A knot formed in the pit of his stomach. "What do you want me to tell them?"

"You might want to start with the truth." She cleared her throat. "There's no way we can make up a story they'll buy at this stage. We got caught, Mac. There isn't any way we can pretty it up so they'll like it."

"The hell there isn't. We could tell them we're in love with each other."

She pulled a T-shirt over her head. "Thanks for the thought, but I'd rather you didn't."

Raw as he felt right now, he didn't have the courage to question her. Maybe she didn't want anyone to know she'd fallen in love with the guy who was merely doing her a service before she left for New York. And the way she was acting right now, he was pretty sure she would go. Maybe she loved him, as she'd said. But she'd leave him anyway.

Without another word, he unlocked the bedroom door and walked down the hall to face his inquisitors.

HE'D BEEN ABOUT to break up with her. Tess fought tears and struggled to get dressed. Oh, he might love her, as he'd said in the heat of passion. He'd probably told several women he loved them over the years, especially when they pleased him sexually. He still hadn't felt the urge to marry one of them. She was just another of his conquests, fun for the summer but not the one he wanted to spend a lifetime with.

There was only one thing Mac could say that would placate her brothers, and that would be to announce their engagement. And he wasn't going to do that.

Angry voices from the direction of the living room told her things weren't going well. Stuffing the harem outfit in a drawer, she ran a brush through her hair and padded barefoot down the hall.

Rhino sounded furious. "So you stand there and admit that you took advantage of our sister's innocent nature?"

Hardly, Tess thought, wondering what sort of story Mac was spinning out there.

"That's exactly what I'm saying." Mac's tone was lower and more controlled. "And if I hadn't, some city slicker in New York would have. She couldn't stay innocent forever, dammit. I convinced her she needed to be prepared before she went off to the big city."

"You *convinced* her?" Hammer bellowed. "You *se-*

duced her, you mean! That poor girl didn't have a chance!"

Tess hurried into the room. "I did so have a chance. I—"

"Tess." Mac turned to her. "You can't assume the responsibility for this. I took advantage of your lack of experience. Simple as that."

"You most certainly did *not*." She realized he was trying to protect her, but she couldn't let him do that. If he had any chance of saving the relationship with her brothers, the truth had to come out. She glanced at her brothers. "I don't know what he told you, but this whole summer project was my idea. I decided back in June that I wanted to lose my virginity before I left for New York."

Rhino and Hammer stared at her, their jaws slack. Rhino was the first to speak. "Summer p-project?"

Mac snorted. "Don't listen to her. You know Tess. She could always make up wild stories on the spur of the moment, and most of the time it was to save my sorry ass. She's doing it again."

"I am not! I came up with my plan and asked Mac if he could fix me up with someone. He offered to take care of it himself."

"Oh, I'll just bet he did!" Rhino advanced on Mac. "And how did she get this idea in the first place, huh? She's never been worried about stuff like that before, so who was putting ideas in her head, buddy-boy?"

Tess stepped between them. "I've been thinking about stuff like that since I was fourteen years old, Rhino! It wasn't Mac's idea, it was mine."

"He probably made you think it was your idea," Hammer said, joining his brother as they faced Mac, fists clenched. "We've always known this is one slick character when it comes to women. We just never thought he'd go behind our backs and prey on our little sister, right, Rhino?"

"That's right. Guess we have to take you outside and work you over, Mac."

"You will not!" Tess pushed a hand into each one of her brothers' substantial chests.

"I can take care of myself, Tess." Mac rolled his shoulders. "You don't have to protect me from your brothers."

"She can't stop us, anyway," Rhino said. He gently nudged Tess aside.

"Yes, I can!" Tess pushed her way between the men again. "If you touch one hair on his head, I'll tell Mom and Dad about the time you guys drove over the border, got drunk on tequila and spent the night in a Nogales jail."

"I don't care," Hammer said. "No biggie."

"And what about the time I found the marijuana in your bedroom, Hammer?" she added sweetly.

"You had pot in your room?" Mac asked. "You never told me that. God, your dad would have had a fit."

A flush spread over Hammer's face. "I only smoked a little of the damn stuff, and it made me puke!"

"So that's what I'll tell the folks," Tess said. "I'm sure they'll understand. Although they might wonder what happened to the rest of the joints, since I found about six."

Hammer's flush deepened. "I sold them at school."

Rhino turned to him, his eyes wide. "You *peddled* those things? You told me you flushed them!"

"Who flushed what?" called out Tim as he came through the front door. "And what's up with the darts tournament? Suzie said you called, so I went and picked up Dozer, but when we got to the Ore Cart they said you'd come down here."

"Yeah," Dozer said, walking in behind Tim. "Are we gonna play or not?"

Rhino crossed his arms over his chest. "It seems somebody's already been playing." He glared at Mac. "Our friend here, the one we all thought we could trust, has been playing house with our sister all summer."

"What?" Dozer looked from Tess to Mac. "Tess, is this true? Did this guy…?"

"It was a mutual decision," Tess said, "so don't go—"

"That's it." Dozer started across the room. "He's toast."

"Hold it, Dozer." Rhino grabbed his brother by the arm. "It's not that simple."

"It *is* simple," Tess said. "I'm the one to blame here, not Mac. I asked him to do this!"

"And he couldn't pronounce the word *no*?" Hammer said.

"I didn't want him to say no! I wanted to finally experience sex!"

Tim's face grew red. "Aw, Tess! What did you have to go and do that for? There's plenty of time for that after you're married!"

"Oh, really?" Tess lifted her chin and surveyed her four brothers. "And I suppose all you guys waited until after you were married?"

There was a general clearing of throats and glancing everywhere but at Tess.

"That's different," Rhino said. "We're guys."

Tess stared at them. "Hello? Can any of you say

women's rights?'' She threw up both arms and paced across the room. "I can't believe we're almost to the millennium and you're still making such outdated statements. In case you hadn't noticed, women aren't considered helpless little flowers anymore."

"Hey, we know all about that stuff," Hammer said. "We got women in the mines now. Women driving the big ore trucks. Women everywhere. But, dammit, Tess, you're our *sister*."

"Yeah, and guys can be real sleazy!" Tim added. "We didn't want you getting hurt or anything! A lot of guys only want to fool around. They're not into the marriage thing."

"Which reminds me of a very critical point." Rhino narrowed his eyes at Mac. "Just what are your plans, now that you've had a real fun summer fooling around with a sweet and innocent young girl?"

"I'm twenty-six, Rhino!"

"That's very young!" Rhino shouted back.

"Not *that* young," Tim said. "I'm twenty-seven."

"We're off the subject," Rhino said. He fixed Mac with an intimidating look. "What are your intentions, Mac?"

Tess panicked. She didn't want to listen to Mac fumble around and try to dodge the question. Suspecting he had no interest in her as a wife was not as bad as hearing him say it. "No plans, folks! *Nada*. Have you forgotten that I'm going to New York in a couple of weeks to start a new job? I'm in no position to make a commitment at this point. In fact, Mac and I had that understanding from the beginning, didn't we, Mac?" If she expected him to look at her with relief and gratitude, she was disappointed.

The blue eyes that had been filled with such passion

not so long ago gazed at her without any expression at all. "Yes, we did."

"That probably suited lover-boy right down to the ground," Hammer muttered. He glanced at Tess. "And I still say you're covering for him and he came up with the idea first. He probably figured this deal was too sweet to pass up—a girl who was leaving town at the end of the summer. Perfect, right, Big Mac?"

Mac's nonchalant shrug broke Tess's heart. That's probably how Mac had thought of their lovemaking. A summer romance. Fun while it lasted. "Well, that was the beauty of it for me, too," she said, forcing the words past a tight throat. "I couldn't afford messy entanglements when I was about to leave."

Rhino looked at her, his gaze far too perceptive. "I don't buy it, Tess."

She squared her shoulders. "Well, I don't give a damn whether you buy it or not. It's the truth."

"Let me get this straight," Dozer said. "On the one hand we have a guy who's been romeoing his way around the county ever since he was fifteen, and on the other we have a girl who's lived like a nun until the age of twenty-six. What—"

"I didn't live like a nun by choice! You guys scared off all my prospects!"

"They were all terrible prospects!" Rhino said.

"And I'm trying to make a point, here," Dozer continued. "Tess says this is all her fault, but I wonder how that could be, considering she had zero experience and the stud-man over here has more experience than anybody in this room. I mean, who do you suppose was in control of that situation?"

"I was!" Tess said.

"Not likely." Dozer started toward Mac again. "And I'm itching to land a few punches."

"Sounds like a plan," Hammer said.

"Might as well get it over with," Rhino added.

Tess grew desperate. She couldn't have her brothers beat up the man she loved. She lowered her voice to deliver her ultimatum. It had always worked for her mother, so maybe it would work for her. "If you do this, I'm through with all of you," she said.

They turned to her with expressions of disbelief.

"I mean it. No brother of mine would gang up on an innocent man. And Mac is innocent."

"Hah!" Dozer said.

Rhino stroked his chin and gazed at her. "Does he mean that much to you, Tess?"

Trapped. There was no answer except the truth. Tears of frustration pushed at the back of her eyes. "Yes, dammit, he does."

Rhino nodded. "Then maybe you ought to stay home and marry him instead of traipsing off to New York."

But he doesn't want that, she longed to say. Instead, she swallowed the lump of emotion in her throat and lied. "Just because you care about someone and don't want them hurt doesn't mean you're ready to give up your dream for them. My dream is to experience some other place besides Copperville, and I finally have the chance to do that." She blinked to hold back the tears.

Rhino studied her for a while longer. "Well, I guess that settles it. We can't very well beat up on Mac and make our sister cry, now, can we?"

"I wouldn't cry." She sniffed. "I just would never speak to you again."

Tim frowned and came over to put a hand on her shoulder. "You look like you might cry."

She sniffed again and glared up at him through swimming eyes. "Well, I won't."

"We've got another thing to think about," Hammer said. "Is this information going to leave this room?"

"No." Rhino fixed each of his brothers with a stern look. "Nobody tells. Not even your wives. Got that?"

Everyone nodded.

Tess gazed at them all with a heavy heart. She wanted this little scene over with. "Don't you all have a darts tournament to play?"

There was a moment of silence. Finally Rhino broke it. "Guess we do. Come on, Mac."

"Thanks," Mac said, "but I think I'll take a pass."

"Like hell you will." Hammer grabbed one of Mac's arms.

"Yeah." Dozer grabbed the other one. "You don't think we'd leave you here, do you?"

"I'll make it even plainer," Rhino said. "Unless Tess changes her mind and decides to marry you, I don't want you around this house again. You may have gotten away with it all summer, but the party's over, buddy. The Blakely brothers are back on duty. Now let's go play some darts."

Tess watched with great misgiving as they escorted Mac out of the house. "You do understand I meant what I said," she called after them as Dozer demanded Mac's keys so he could drive Mac's truck. "If you hurt him, I'll find out, and there will be hell to pay."

"We won't hurt him, Tess," Rhino promised as he climbed into his truck. "We just won't let him within ten feet of you ever again."

15

MAC WISHED the Blakely brothers *had* started swinging at him once they were out of Tess's sight. A nice little brawl would have been an improvement over what was happening at the Ore Cart. As he sat at the bar and nursed a beer, he wondered if they were trying to get him to throw the first punch. He wasn't about to do it.

He felt numb, which was another reason he'd love to get in a fight just so he could at least feel something and know he was still alive. But he wouldn't be the one to start it. Like someone in shock staring down at a gaping wound, he should be feeling tremendous pain knowing that he'd never hold Tess in his arms again. He had no doubt he would feel that pain eventually. But the reality of losing his best friend and the love of his life hadn't hit him yet.

"Hey, Benedict Arnold, you're up." Hammer pulled the darts he'd just thrown from the board and handed them to Mac, points out.

Mac took them, gazing stoically at Hammer as one of the points seemed to accidentally dig into his palm. "Thanks."

"Whoops, did I stick you with that dart? Jeez, I'm sorry, man. Oversight on my part."

"No problem."

"Check where he's putting his feet," Dozer said. "A

guy like him could edge over the line to get an advantage."

"I'm watching him," Rhino said. "All the time."

Mac clenched his jaw and threw the darts. He sensed that the brothers were testing him, trying to get him to crack. If he challenged them, either by starting a fight or leaving the bar, that would be the end of the relationship. If he stayed and took everything they had to dish out, the day of forgiveness might eventually come.

Unfortunately he was starting to win the damn darts tournament. Throwing darts felt exceedingly good right now. He'd give anything to be out on the field throwing a football right now. He could probably heave it seventy yards with no problem. He deliberately made a bad toss of the dart.

"Hey, lover-boy!" Dozer called out. "Having a little trouble with your concentration?"

"No doubt," Rhino said. "The boy has a lot of things on his mind. No wonder he hasn't been winning at poker this summer."

"I still can't believe it," Tim said. He of all the brothers seemed more hurt than angry. "I can't believe you'd sit there every Wednesday night like always."

"Sort of makes you lose your faith in your fellow man, doesn't it, Tim?" Hammer said.

Mac threw his last dart dead in the middle of the bull's-eye and turned to face the brothers. He gazed at them and pain started sneaking into his heart, like the pinpricks after an arm or leg has fallen asleep. Nothing would ever be the same. Nothing. "I'm sorry," he said softly.

They returned his gaze silently.

Finally Tim spoke. "Would you marry her if she wasn't going to New York, Mac?"

He saw nothing wrong with telling them the truth. "Yes."

Rhino made an impatient noise deep in his throat. "Then why the hell don't you get her to stay?"

"I don't think I could," Mac said.

"You could," Rhino said. "She might pretend she's one of those women who takes her fun where she finds it, but she's not. We always figured she'd fall hard for the first guy she got involved with because she's not the type to take sex lightly, no matter what she says. That's the main reason we've been protecting her all along. She could have wrecked her life with the wrong guy."

"Maybe I'm the wrong guy."

Hammer drained his glass of beer and set it down on the bar with a loud click. "Maybe. I can't say I'd relish having a lying son of a bitch for a brother-in-law."

"He didn't exactly lie," Tim said.

"No, it's more like he betrayed our trust," Rhino said. "Now, that's not good, but I'm telling you, Tess has probably lost her heart, just like we thought she would when she became involved with someone. I think you need to convince her to stay here and marry you, Mac. It's the only answer."

Mac considered the idea, and for a brief moment hope gleamed in his heart. He knew Tess loved him. If only she'd given him some indication that she didn't really want to go to New York...but she hadn't.

He took a deep breath. "You're right, I might be able to convince her to stay. But I can't do it. All her life she's talked about leaving small-town life behind and experiencing the excitement of a big city. She could

easily start blaming me for taking that away from her."
He should know. Despite how much he loved his parents, he couldn't completely eliminate the resentment that cropped up whenever he thought of how they'd tied him to the ranch.

"Hell. You have a point." Rhino gazed at the floor. "I hate this. I purely hate it. If you were some other guy, we could all have a great time taking you apart."

Mac laid the darts on the bar. "Have at it."

"We can't beat you up, Mac," Tim said. "Not after the way you said you were sorry, and that you'd marry Tess if you thought it would work out."

"Maybe it would work out," Dozer said. "Maybe she'd forget about this big-city thing after a while. Like the sofa Cindy wanted. She thought she'd die if she didn't get it, but we couldn't afford the darn thing. Then after she got pregnant she forgot about the sofa."

Mac's smile was sad. "I wish you were right, Dozer. But I've listened to Tess go on about this for years. You guys got so much recognition with your football that she felt overshadowed most of the time."

"Yeah, but she was in those plays," Tim said.

"I know, but Copperville folks don't get as excited about plays as they do about football games. You know she once considered trying to make it on Broadway."

Rhino groaned. "We were all having a heart attack over that plan, too."

"That Broadway idea was because of us?" Dozer asked.

"In a way. It would have made a splash. At any rate, thinking about a career on Broadway got her hooked on the idea of New York, but she finally realized she didn't want to act for a living, so she decided to get a job in New York as the next best thing. Because no one else in the family has done anything remotely like that, it'll be her badge of honor. I think she needs to go."

"I can't believe she's been jealous of us, when she was so smart, pulling down A's all the time," Hammer said.

"Pulling down A's doesn't rate a picture in the paper. Don't get me wrong. She's proud as heck of all of you, but she wants her own claim to fame. This is it."

Rhino stroked his chin. "You seem to know her pretty well."

Hammer coughed. "A little too damn well, if you want my opinion. Why didn't you just tell her you wouldn't do it, Mac?"

"I should have. God, I know I should have. But she seemed so determined to make this happen. She was considering Donny Beauford."

A strangled noise came from Rhino, and Dozer choked on his beer.

"God bless America," Hammer said. "Beauford?"

"I'd ten times rather have Mac than Beauford," Tim said. "Make that a hundred times."

A silence fell over the brothers as each of them seemed to be contemplating the horrors of Donny Beauford with their sister.

"I guess it had to be somebody, sooner or later," Tim said at last.

"We knew that," Rhino said. "But we wanted to make sure it was the right guy."

"I've been wondering about something," Mac said. "How were you planning to supervise Tess's dating life once she moved to New York?"

Rhino grinned. "We had a special picture made of all four of us and we planned to give it to her as a going-away present."

"And we had the photographer squat and point the camera up, so we all look *huge*," Tim added.

"We're going to tell her to keep it right by her bedside to remind her of her family," Dozer said. "Any guy who sees that might think twice, especially if we pay a few surprise visits to New York now and then."

Mac shook his head. "Amazing."

"We might not have to worry so much now," Rhino said. "If we want to look on the bright side of this disaster, Mac might have done us a favor."

Hammer glared at Mac. "I can't buy that."

"Think about it," Rhino said. "You know how she is once she settles on someone or something. Like a little bulldog. If she's carrying a torch for Mac, she won't be interested in any of those city slickers."

Mac thought that was one of the best things he'd heard all night. Unfortunately it didn't change the fact that Tess would be leaving and he would be staying. His life was about to become very empty, more empty than he could imagine. So if he wanted to keep his sanity, he wouldn't even try to imagine life without Tess.

TESS KNEW that her last two weeks in Copperville would be rough, but she hadn't understood the half of it. She ached from wanting Mac, but she'd expected that. The need for him was always there, a subterranean current that sometimes bubbled to the surface and threatened to drown her. But the moments she hadn't expected were worse—moments when her first impulse was to share some little detail of her life with Mac, until she realized she could no longer do that.

There was the time she rescued Sarah's kitten from a tree, and the hysterical sight of Mrs. Nedbetter riding around on her new mower, even though she had a postage-stamp lawn. Tess would hear a good joke or read an article about a new technique for breeding horses, and pick up the phone. And then the truth would hit her. No matter what he'd promised about always being friends, their friendship was dead.

The most exquisite torture of all lay ahead of her. Her parents' anniversary party was no longer a surprise—surprises seldom worked out in Copperville. Once the secret was out, her family had decided to combine an anniversary barbecue in the park with a going-away party for Tess. Most of the population of Copperville would be there…including Mac.

By the day of the party, Tess had packed most of her belongings, including many of her clothes. Too late she realized that the only thing she hadn't packed that was festive enough for the event was her daisy-patterned dress. Mac would probably think she'd worn it on purpose. The only reason it still hung in her closet was that she hadn't gotten around to stuffing it in the bag of discards she'd collected to give to charity.

As she zipped the dress, she realized that the pearl necklace she'd continued to wear probably would be another red flag for Mac. For the past two weeks she kept meaning to take it off for good, although she couldn't make herself give it away. But each time she'd reached for the clasp so she could put the necklace back into her jewelry box, she'd decided to leave it on a little longer.

Putting the necklace away seemed so final, as if that would sever the last tie with Mac. Besides, her mother had mentioned how nice she thought it was that Tess was finally wearing the lovely gift Mac had given her. Her mother might notice the necklace was gone and comment, Tess decided. Better to leave it on. Mac would just have to deal with it.

She arrived at the park early to help her brothers and sisters-in-law with the preparations. They worked steadily for two hours in the heat, tying balloons to lampposts, firing up the barbecue grills and chasing rambunctious children. Tess welcomed the sweaty, frantic activity and pushed thoughts of Mac to the back of her mind.

But her pulse started to race right on schedule when he backed his truck up to a ramada and started unloading the kegs of beer that had been ordered for the party.

"Guess I'll go help him," Rhino said.

"Don't sample the wares until we're finished here," Joan called after her husband.

Tess kept sneaking glances at the two men as they laughed and joked with each other while unloading the kegs. Pretty soon Hammer, Dozer and Tim wandered over and joined them. Everyone acted like the best of buddies, and she began to hope that her brothers had made a temporary peace with Mac. Once she wasn't around, they might be able to put the whole incident aside.

"Hey, Dozer," Cindy called over to the group. "Time for you and Tim to start cooking. People are beginning to arrive and the anniversary couple will be here any minute."

"Coming," Dozer said.

Deena continued tying the last of the balloons on an adjacent ramada. "Hammer," she called. "I need you to check on Jason and Kimberly at the swings. Suzie's been playing with them over there, but I'll bet she could use a breather."

Hammer headed toward the swings. "Jason, let Kimberly have a turn, son!"

Tess pretended not to notice that Mac had tagged along as Tim, Dozer and Rhino approached the table. Instead, she concentrated on filling a large wading pool with ice to hold the salad bowls. She'd never followed through on her plan to use ice during lovemaking with Mac, but ice never failed to remind her of the passionate adventures they'd shared this summer.

"Cindy, which cooler did you put the hamburgers and hot dogs in?" Dozer asked.

"The red one," Cindy said.

"*Which* red one?"

"Oh, for heaven's sake." Cindy got Dozer by one arm and Tim by the other and propelled them over to a nearby ramada. "Come on. I'll show you."

Tess dumped the last bag of ice in the wading pool. "This is ready, Joan."

"For what?" Mac asked.

Tess glanced at him and could tell by the challenging look in his eyes that he'd meant for the question to rattle her. It did. Her cheeks warmed. "We, uh—"

"It's for the salads, so you don't get poisoned by the mayonnaise," Joan said briskly.

"That's not all it's for." Rhino grabbed a piece of ice and slipped it down the back of Joan's dress.

She shrieked and scooped up a handful of ice, pelting him with it as she chased him across the park.

And just like that, Mac and Tess were alone.

He picked up an ice cube and tossed it up and down in his hand. "We never did get around to this, did we?"

Her throat felt so tight that she couldn't speak. She shook her head.

"Guess we never will." He tossed the ice on the ground and moved closer. "How are you doing?"

"Okay." She risked one look into his eyes and glanced away again. Too potent. She cleared the huskiness from her throat. "How about you?"

"Okay. I thought about calling you to see how you were holding up, but I thought that might make things worse."

"Yeah. It probably would have." She watched the ice cube melt in the grass at their feet. "Mac, did my brothers—"

"Beat me up? No. In a way I wish they had. It might have made me feel better."

Tess glanced across the park. Joan and Rhino were walking back toward them. They didn't have much time. She lowered her voice. "Dammit, I will not have you taking the blame for this. It was my idea and I should be the one feeling guilty, not you."

"Like they said, I could have turned you down."

"You knew I was going to nab somebody for the job, and you were afraid I'd end up with a dweeb."

"Yeah. And then there was that dress."

She glanced at him.

"Why did you wear it today, Tess?"

Because I was selfish enough to want you to look at me like that one more time. "I'd packed everything else."

"And what about the necklace?" he asked softly. "Didn't get around to packing that, either, did you?"

Her heart ached so fiercely she could barely breathe. "Mac, I—"

"Promise me something."

"What?"

"That you'll wear that necklace in New York."

"Loafing, are we?" Joan said with a grin as they

walked up. "Boy, I can't leave my staff for a minute without discipline going to hell."

Rhino's glance shifted from Mac to Tess and he frowned. "I'll put Big Mac to work for you, sweetheart. He's probably distracting Tess so she can't get anything done."

"Oh, I don't really care," Joan said. "After all, we won't have Tess around here much longer, so I'm sure everybody wants a chance to spend a little time with her today. Technically, I shouldn't be making her work at all, since this is also supposed to be her party."

"I wouldn't feel right sitting around," Tess said. She'd caught the brief look of disapproval on her brother's face. He might have shelved his anger for the time being, but he wasn't about to let Mac spend any more time alone with her.

"None of us are going to sit around," Rhino said. "Come on, Mac. I have a bunch of lawn chairs in the van. Let's go take them out and set them up."

"Sure thing." Mac glanced at Tess.

She realized she was clutching the pearl in one hand. She released it and turned away. His request completely confused her. He knew that wearing the necklace would be a constant reminder of him, preventing her from moving on to someone else. That sort of dog-in-the-manger attitude wasn't worthy of him, and she couldn't quite believe that was his motivation. Yet she could think of no other reason he'd want her to continue wearing the necklace.

The more she thought about it, the angrier she became. Who did he think he was, branding her like that when he didn't have the slightest intention of making a commitment himself?

Her parents arrived soon afterward. Once the party

was in full swing, Tess focused on making this a special day for her parents. More than once she felt the tug of tears as she realized that by next week she wouldn't be able to see them and talk to them every day as she could now. She wondered if she'd made a terrible mistake taking the job in New York, but she couldn't change her course now, and besides, she needed to get away from Mac. If she stayed around much longer, he would surely break her heart for good.

Although the festivities took most of her attention, she couldn't forget that Mac was there, although she really tried. Despite her efforts, she always seemed to know where he was, whether he'd stripped off his shirt for the volleyball game, or had taken yet another kid for a ride on his shoulders, or was challenging one of her brothers to a game of horseshoes. His voice, his smile, his laughter drew her as if they were connected with an invisible string.

Finally she decided the pearl necklace was part of the problem. She couldn't take it to New York, let alone wear it while she was there. And Mac needed to know that.

She excused herself on the pretext that she needed to head for one of the park rest rooms. When she was away from the crowd, she took off the necklace. Unclasping it wasn't easy because her hands were shaking. Once she'd done it, she felt as if someone had wrapped her heart in barbed wire.

But this was what she had to do. She found Mac eating some of her parents' anniversary cake while he talked with a couple of ranchers who lived on the outskirts of Copperville.

"Excuse me, Mac," she said.

"Sure." He glanced at her bare neck and his gaze grew wary. "What is it?"

She reached over and dropped the necklace in his shirt pocket. "I need you to keep this for me." Choking back a sob, she turned and hurried away.

16

MAC WANTED to throw the necklace away. In the tortured days that followed, right up to the morning Tess
was scheduled to leave, he tried to make himself pitch
it in the garbage, in the river, over a cliff. He couldn't
do it.

The day she left, he drove to a bluff overlooking the
highway winding out of town and waited there until
he saw her car go by. He thought he'd fling the necklace over the bluff once he knew she was really and
truly gone. But long after her car and trailer had disappeared from sight, he still clutched the necklace tight
in his fist.

In the weeks that followed he kept the necklace in a
drawer and fell into the habit of tucking it into his
jeans' pocket before starting the day. He'd meant for
her to keep it on as a reminder of him and what they'd
meant to each other. He'd held on to the slim hope that
after some time of living in the big city she'd grow tired
of it and come home. If she wore the necklace until
then, he might have a chance. But she'd turned the
tables on him...again.

He handled his ranch duties like a robot. The work
had always seemed confining to him, but he'd been
able to bear it while Tess remained in Copperville.
Now the daily routine was intolerable without her.
She'd been the one who had kept his life interesting,

and the fact that she shared his desire to go out into the world had kept that fantasy alive for him. Now she was out there and he was left behind.

As the heat lifted in late September, he was rounding up strays down by the river one afternoon when he came to a life-changing realization. Once his parents were gone, he'd sell the ranch and travel the world. That wouldn't take the place of losing Tess, but it would have to do. And if he was planning to sell the ranch eventually anyway, his parents' dream of keeping it in the family and passing it down through the generations was doomed from the beginning.

Suddenly the whole charade seemed stupid. To pretend he wanted a ranch that he wouldn't keep after his parents died was unfair to all of them. Telling his mom and dad the truth after all these years wouldn't be easy, though. Still, he was determined to do it and end the hypocrisy.

He waited until dinner was nearly over. He'd barely been able to taste his mother's prized beef stew, but he'd forced himself to eat every bite and carry on a conversation about the antics of the stud they'd bought from Stan Henderson in Flagstaff.

From the moment he'd come into the ranch house that night he'd seen the place with new eyes. Now that he'd decided the ranch would not be his ball and chain, he could appreciate the beamed ceilings and rock fireplace, the heavy leather furniture grouped around the hearth and the carved oak table and chairs in the dining room.

It wouldn't be such a bad place to live...someday, and with the right person. But he couldn't expect his parents to keep it going without him, holding on to it for when he was ready to settle down. And before that day came, he had many things to do.

Finally he pushed his plate aside and gazed at them. "I need to talk to both of you. It's...pretty serious."

"At last," his mother said with a sigh.

Mac stared at her. "What do you mean, *at last?*"

"Your mother's been worried sick about you ever since Tess left," his father said. "I've been a mite concerned, myself. You've been moping around like you've lost your best friend, and I guess you have."

Mac felt his neck grow warm. It showed how self-absorbed he'd been lately, that he hadn't even realized how his mood had been affecting his parents. "I'm sorry if I've been a pain in the butt."

"You have," his father said.

"No, he hasn't, Andy." Nora sent her husband a reproving glance. "He's been sort of glum, that's all."

"Which translates to being a pain in the butt, in my opinion," Andy said.

"I agree," Mac said. "But I'm about to be even more of one." He took a deep breath. "I know you've both worked hard all these years to build up this ranch."

"It's been a labor of love," his mother said.

She wasn't making it any easier for him. Mac cleared his throat. "I appreciate all that you've done, and I realize the goal was to pass the ranch on to me someday, but—"

"You don't want it," his father finished, his voice husky.

Mac met his father's gaze and his resolve nearly crumbled at the deep disappointment he saw there. "I might," he said gently. "Eventually, when I get some of the wanderlust out of my system. It's a beautiful place, and tonight I really began to realize just how beautiful it is. But right now the ranch feels like an elephant sitting on my chest, choking the life out of me."

"You want to go to New York, don't you?" his mother asked quietly.

"Maybe." *Yes.* He hadn't allowed himself to get that far in his thinking, but now that his mother had put the idea into words, he knew immediately that he wanted to start with New York. He wasn't sure how Tess figured into any of this, or if she even wanted to figure in, but he would never know if he didn't go there and find out.

"What in hell would you do in New York?" his father asked. His tone of voice betrayed the depth of his hurt.

"I'm not sure." The ideas started coming to him, and he realized they'd been simmering in his subconscious for years. "I'd probably try to get on with one of the small commuter airlines there. If that didn't pan out I'd find some job at one of the major airports and work my way up until I could fly. I love airplanes, Dad. I always have."

"You have a damn airplane! You can fly it around all you want!"

"Andy." Nora laid a hand on her husband's arm. "That's not the point. He wants to go out on his own, the way Tess has. Plus, he misses her like crazy. I don't know if something more than friendship is involved, but I'm beginning to think there is." She glanced at Mac. "I didn't want to interfere, but I had a strong feeling that you and Tess went beyond the boundaries of friendship this summer. Debbie thought so, too."

"You and Tess's mom talked about it?" Mac felt the heat climb from his neck to his face.

"To be honest, a lot of people in town had their suspicions," his mother said. "We wondered if Tess might decide to stay home, after all. When she left, I felt so bad for you."

"I knew it." Andy threw his napkin on the table and pushed back his chair. "This is all about chasing after a woman. If Tess had had the good sense to stay in Copperville, then you two could get married and you wouldn't be comparing the ranch to some damn elephant."

"Don't blame it on Tess!" In his agitation, Mac rose to his feet. "I've always felt this way. Both of us have, Tess and I. We spent hours as kids talking about the places we'd see, the exciting things we'd do once we left Copperville."

"Lots of kids talk that way," his father said. "Then they grow up and realize that what they have is better than anything they could find out there!"

Mac gazed at his father and tried to put himself in Andy MacDougal's shoes. After nearly thirty years of breaking his back to create a legacy for his son, his son was rejecting that legacy. Mac hated hurting his father. "It probably is better, Dad," he said gently. "But I'll never appreciate that if I don't see something of the rest of the world."

"Of course you must," his mother said.

"Maybe we should just sell the ranch right now," Andy said. "No point in killing ourselves if it's not going to be passed on."

"Oh, Andy, for heaven's sake!" Nora looked disgusted. "Forget your hurt pride for five seconds and listen to what your son is saying. He needs time to explore. And he needs to be with the woman he loves."

Mac's heart clutched. "Now, Mom. Don't jump to—"

"I'll jump to any conclusion I want, thank you very much." She glanced at him. "And Tess feels the same about you, unless I miss my guess. I also fully believe that both of you will eventually get homesick for Copperville and come back here to raise your children."

"Children?" Mac almost choked. "Last I heard, Tess had no intention of getting married, let alone having kids. I think you're getting ahead of yourself."

His mother smiled. "No, I think you're behind. Time to catch up. Go to New York and ask those questions. See what kind of response you get." She looked over at her husband. "All we need to do is hire someone to help out for a while, until these two come back home."

Andy scowled. "And what if they don't? Then it'll all be for nothing."

"Now that's the dumbest thing I've ever heard you say, Andy. Nothing? This ranch was your dream all along. You hoped it would be passed down, as a lot of parents do who work to build something, but you wanted it for yourself, too. You've had a wonderful time living this life, and don't you dare pretend it was nothing but selfless sacrifice for your son!"

Gradually Andy's expression changed from belligerent to sheepish. "Guess you're right, Nora. I can't imagine any other place to be. That's why I can't figure why anybody in their right mind would want to live in that rat's nest they call New York City."

"We're all different," Nora said. "As for these two, they were both born and raised here, and I say they'll be back."

"I can't make any promises," Mac said. But he couldn't help weaving a few fantasies, either. Maybe he could have it all, a few years of adventures with Tess and then a family and security right here in Copperville with the only woman he'd ever wanted. But Tess might not be interested in such a plan. After all, she had given back the necklace.

"You don't have to make any promises to us," his mother said. "But I think you need to make a few to Tess."

NEW YORK WAS EVERYTHING Tess had imagined and more. She'd used her weekends to walk Manhattan from end to end, and each excursion brought new delights. She'd become addicted to pretzels sold by sidewalk vendors, and corner deli markets, and the ride up to the top of the Empire State Building.

But she'd never expected to be so completely, utterly lonely. She'd made friends with people on the staff of her school, but *friend* didn't seem like the right word to describe someone she'd only known a couple of months. Friends were people you'd known for years, people who knew your family and all your other friends. Friends were people like…Mac.

She'd thought the ache for him would have begun to wear away by now, but if anything, it grew stronger. Today was worse than most days, because it was both Sunday, a time for families, and Halloween, a holiday she and Mac had shared for twenty-three years. They'd never considered themselves too old to dress up. A year ago they'd gone to a party together as a couple of Beanie Babies.

Tess had been invited to a party given by one of the teachers at school, and she'd accepted, but as she sat in her tiny apartment trying to come up with a costume, she couldn't get excited about it. Her simplest option was to wear the harem outfit she'd bought for the belly-dancing demonstration she'd given Mac. She thought she'd thrown it away, but she must have been in a real fog when she'd packed, because it was in the bottom of a box. Once she discovered it, she'd been so desperate for any reminders of Mac that she'd kept it.

Wearing it, however, might present a few emotional problems. Yet she didn't have any other great ideas for a costume, and this one was complete. With a sigh she started putting it on for a test run to see whether it made her cry, or worse yet made her hot and bothered. Sexual frustration had been a constant companion along with loneliness, but of the two, loneliness was the worst. She missed having Mac to talk to even more than she missed his lovemaking.

Still, she'd give anything to be held and caressed by him again, and it was definitely *his* lovemaking that she wanted. She'd turned down several dates already. The thought of even kissing someone besides Mac made her shudder.

If that attitude persisted, she might have to resign herself to staying single all her life. Damned if she wasn't beginning to believe she was a one-man woman. She'd never have believed it before the scorching events of this summer, but it seemed that Mac had taken not only her virginity, but her heart. And she wasn't getting it back.

After putting on the filmy harem pants and the jeweled bra, she stood in front of the mirror in her small bedroom and fastened the veil in place. Heat washed over her as she remembered the look in Mac's eyes as she'd danced for him. She'd never felt so sensuous as when she'd leaned over him and shimmied her breasts practically in his face.

He'd meant to end their affair that night without making love to her, but she'd tempted him beyond endurance and even made him forget he'd agreed to meet her brothers for a darts tournament. In all the turmoil that had followed, she'd forgotten that her seductive dance had succeeded beyond her wildest dreams. She had made him lose his mind. Maybe he didn't want to marry her, but for that moment, he had been completely, utterly hers.

And he'd said that he loved her. It had turned out to be an empty pledge, and now she wondered if he'd only meant that he loved the fantastic sex they'd made together. But when he'd said it that night, he'd filled her heart to overflowing.

She couldn't wear the harem outfit to the Halloween party. It made her long for Mac in every conceivable way—physically, mentally and emotionally. Maybe she'd skip the party altogether and rent a video. She reached for the hook on the jeweled bra just as the doorbell rang.

Probably her next-door neighbor, she thought. She'd moved clear across the country, yet some things stayed the same. The woman in the next apartment reminded her so much of her neighbor, Mrs. Nedbetter, back in Copperville, that several times she'd called her by the wrong name.

She glanced at herself in the mirror. Oh, well, it was Halloween. She'd explain that she was trying on costumes in preparation for a party. She really should make herself go, she thought as she walked toward the front door. A simple costume like a gypsy or a pirate wouldn't be that hard to create.

The doorbell chimed again. Then a voice that made her breath catch called out "Trick or treat."

"Mac!" She raced to the door and unlocked it, fumbling in her eagerness. So what if he'd only come for a visit and would leave her worse off than she was now? She didn't care. She flung open the door and gasped.

He was dressed as a sheik, complete with rich-looking robes and a gold piece of braid holding a white flowing turban on his head. When he saw her, his jaw dropped. "Wow. This is just plain scary."

"Yeah." She held his gaze, her heart pounding. "Scary as hell."

"Are you going to a Halloween party?"

"No. Well, maybe. I was invited and I was trying to decide if I wanted to go or not, so I put this on in case I could wear it." She gulped for air. "But I can't."

"Funny, but you seem to be wearing it. Or is that an optical illusion?"

"I—listen, come in." She stepped back from the door. "Do you have bags? How long can you stay? When did you—"

"No bags. I left them at the hotel."

Her hopes died. "H-hotel? You're not…planning to stay…with me?"

He walked through the doorway, his sheik's robes swaying, and closed the door behind him. Then he turned to her. "I didn't want to impose on you. I'm sure you have all sorts of things going on."

So he had come for a visit, with a capital *V*. He probably wanted someone to show him the sights, and she was handy, but he'd distanced himself from her by checking into a hotel. His sheik's outfit was a little joke, not a significant statement of his intentions.

"Well, of course I have things going on." She was determined to hide her pain. "But I'd be glad to adjust my schedule. If you'd told me you were coming, I might have been able to arrange a couple of days off, but on short notice, I'm not sure."

He waved a hand as if that didn't matter to him. "I don't want you to interrupt your work for me." He hesitated. "You said you were invited to a party." His voice became husky. "Do you have a date?"

For a split second she considered lying, but she'd never been good at that, especially with Mac. "No. It's just some people from work. Not a couples sort of thing."

"And you're thinking of going in *that?*"

She bristled. Deciding not to wear it because of the memories it evoked was one thing. Having him question her choice in that tone of voice was quite another. He didn't have that right. "Why not?"

"Because it's indecent!"

"You didn't think so that night I danced for you!" She blew the veil impatiently away from her face. "You enjoyed this outfit so much your tongue was hanging out, mister!"

"And it still is! And so will every other guy's at that party!"

Her chin lifted. "What's it to you?"

He stepped forward and grabbed her. "Everything."

Her breath caught as the space surrounding them seemed to glow and pulse. She became lost in his gaze.

He squeezed his eyes shut. "Damn. I didn't mean it to come out like that."

"You didn't?" Some of the luster faded.

"No." He looked into her eyes. "I meant to go slow, find out if you had a boyfriend."

The luster returned.

"Well?" he prompted.

Wherever this conversation was leading she wanted

to go along, but he'd taken his time about having this talk with her. She decided not to make it too easy and ruin the challenge for him. "Well, what?"

"Do you have a boyfriend?"

What a beautiful day. What an absolutely gorgeous day. "I think so."

"You *think* so?" He scowled down at her. "What kind of an answer is that?"

She was glad she still wore the veil. It hid her smile. "He's not being real clear about his intentions, so it's hard for me to know whether he's my boyfriend or not. But I'm pretty sure he is."

Mac's scowl darkened. "So he's one of those wishy-washy types?"

"Let's just say he's a little confused."

"And how do you feel about him?"

"I'm crazy about him."

His eyes blazed and his grip tightened on her arms. "You can't be."

"Why not? He's terrific."

"Terrific? What do you mean by that?" His eyes narrowed. "Tess, have you and this guy...made love?"

"Not recently."

"I don't give a damn if it's recent or not! Tess, how could you make love to another man? How could you—"

"In fact, I haven't made love to this guy since August," she added gently. "I was wearing this outfit at the time."

Understanding slowly softened the fierce line of his eyebrows and the glitter in his blue eyes. "Oh." He swallowed. "Did I hear you say you're crazy about this guy?"

She nodded.

"I can't imagine why." His voice was hoarse. "He's an idiot."

"No." She reached up and touched his cheek. "Just confused." She stroked the curve of his jaw with a trembling hand. She wanted him, no matter how long he could stay or what his terms might be. "Would you like to cancel that hotel reservation? No one in Copperville has to know that you stayed here during your visit, if that's what you're worried about."

"I'm not visiting."

"What?"

"I'm job hunting, looking into a couple of commuter airlines. I've come here to live."

She reeled from the news. "Mac! What about the ranch? What about your parents?"

"They've hired someone to take over my part of the work. Telling them that I needed to go out on my own wasn't easy, but it was the right thing to do. I should have told them sooner, but I guess I needed you to blaze a trail for me."

"I'm stunned."

His eyes grew shadowed. "Look, this puts you under no obligation. I'm not asking you to change your life just because I decided to come here. I mean, sure, I'd like to see you, and everything, but—"

"And what do you mean exactly by *and everything*?" She moved her hips boldly against his and felt his instantaneous response. "This?"

He groaned softly. "Tess, I—"

"And this?" She pushed the material of his sheik's robe aside and brushed her jeweled bra against his bare chest.

His gaze smoldered. "You drive me insane, Tess. I've missed you so much I can barely think straight."

She pressed her body against his. "If you can't think straight, then maybe you don't remember what you told me when we made love that last time."

"Oh, I remember that, all right."

She gathered her courage and continued. "I need to know if it was just something you said in the heat of passion, or if it meant more than that."

He held her tighter. "You want all my cards on the table, don't you?"

"Yes."

"Then take off that damn veil."

She reached up and unfastened it immediately, tossing it to a nearby chair.

He gazed down at her, his glance warm as it roved over her face. Then he reached beneath his robe and pulled out the pearl necklace. "I think it's time you put this back on."

Her heart thudded wildly at the implication. She trembled as he fastened the clasp around her neck and nestled the pearl between her breasts.

"Okay," he said softly. "I was going to lead up to this, but if you want everything all at once, that's what you'll get. I love you. Maybe on some level I've always known you were my mate, but so many things got in the way. I'm going to marry you someday, Tess, when you're ready. I realize that might not be for a while, but—"

"I'm ready."

"I'm willing to wait until you've experienced all…" He paused, as if finally registering what she'd said. He looked into her eyes.

She nodded.

"Oh, God." His mouth came down on hers, and he kissed her until they were both breathless. "You're sure?" He held her face in both hands, his gaze probing. "I mean, you just started this new life, and maybe you need to stay single for a couple of years, to—"

"To what? Nothing could be as exciting as living with you as your wife. I think I've known that since I was three years old. I love you, Mac, desperately, completely and forever."

His smile was tender. "Yeah, but do you swear on the tomb of old King Tut?"

"You bet. And now let me give you some vital information. The bedroom is through that door on your right. Do you think we could go in there and make mad, passionate love for about ten hours? I'm feeling very neglected."

He grinned and lifted her up in his arms. "Only ten hours?"

"For starters."

He feathered his lips over hers. "Got ice?" he murmured.

Epilogue

PLEASANTLY FULL after a meal of fried chicken and potato salad, Mac lay back on the picnic blanket, closed his eyes and sighed with contentment. No New York traffic, no jackhammers, no jet engines. Only the gurgle of the river, the call of a quail, the rustle of the breeze through the reeds.

He'd visited beaches and riverbanks in many parts of the world this past year, but he'd recognize the baked-sand and wet-moss scent of this one blindfolded. The breeze moved over him like a caress. How he loved summer nights in Arizona.

Something tickled his nose, and he swatted it away. The tickling resumed, and he opened one eye.

Leaning over him, Tess brushed a feathery tip of a wild-grass stalk over his mouth.

He gazed up and noticed that when she leaned over, her blouse gaped open quite nicely. Taking the stalk from her fingers, he slipped it down the front of her blouse and stroked it over the swell of her breasts. "They already seem fuller."

"It's probably your imagination. I'm barely three months along."

"I'll never forget the look on our folks' faces when we told them." He could see desire stirring in her eyes as he continued to tickle her breasts with the grass.

She smiled. "I think they were even happier about

the baby than when we told them we were home to stay."

"I'm pretty happy about that baby, myself." He brushed the grass up the curve of her throat and tickled under her chin. "Any regrets about leaving the big city?"

"Only that we never did it on top of the Empire State Building."

"We'll visit someday and do it then."

She shook her head. "Nah. We don't have to. Making love to you for the rest of my life is all the adventure I need."

"You mean that?"

"Absolutely."

"Then take off your blouse," he murmured. The sight of Tess unfastening buttons was one of the joys of his life.

She obliged him and tossed the garment aside before gazing down at him, a question in her gray eyes.

"Keep going." His erection strained his jeans as she flipped open the front catch of her bra. In another moment her breasts spilled into view, her nipples already taut. He stroked the grass across them anyway, loving the ripple of desire that went through her, the surrender in her sigh.

His voice grew husky. "Lean down."

She moved over him and he filled both hands with the weight of her breasts, kneading gently as he began to taste her.

While he feasted, she managed to wiggle out of her shorts, open his jeans and free his erection. He groaned with pleasure as she slid down over his rigid shaft. How miraculous to make love this way, without barriers. Releasing her breasts, he guided her down for a long, satisfying kiss.

She drew back and gazed into his eyes as she initiated a slow, sensuous rhythm. "I love you, Mac."

"And I love you," he said. Above her the cottonwood leaves dappled the twilight sky. Heaven couldn't be any better than this. "I love you more than life." His climax was building quickly, and from the way Tess was breathing, she wasn't far behind him.

"Stop," she said, panting. "I just remembered."

His fevered brain wasn't working. "Remembered what?"

"Hold on a sec." She reached toward the small picnic cooler near the edge of the blanket.

He squeezed his eyes shut, teetering on the edge. "I don't know if I can." He felt the pulsing begin. "Tess, I can't—" Something cold pressed against a critical part of his anatomy and he erupted, sensations crashing over him in waves, ripping moans of ecstasy from deep in his chest.

Finally he lay still, spent and quivering, while she sprinkled kisses over his face.

"What...was that?" he asked.

She sounded very smug. "Ice."

If you enjoyed what you just read,
then we've got an offer you can't resist!

Take 2 bestselling love stories FREE!
Plus get a FREE surprise gift!

Clip this page and mail it to Harlequin Reader Service®

IN U.S.A.
3010 Walden Ave.
P.O. Box 1867
Buffalo, N.Y. 14240-1867

IN CANADA
P.O. Box 609
Fort Erie, Ontario
L2A 5X3

YES! Please send me 2 free Harlequin Temptation® novels and my free surprise gift. Then send me 4 brand-new novels every month, which I will receive months before they're available in stores. In the U.S.A., bill me at the bargain price of $3.12 plus 25¢ delivery per book and applicable sales tax, if any*. In Canada, bill me at the bargain price of $3.57 plus 25¢ delivery per book and applicable taxes**. That's the complete price and a savings of over 10% off the cover prices—what a great deal! I understand that accepting the 2 free books and gift places me under no obligation ever to buy any books. I can always return a shipment and cancel at any time. Even if I never buy another book from Harlequin, the 2 free books and gift are mine to keep forever. So why not take us up on our invitation. You'll be glad you did!

142 HEN CNEV
342 HEN CNEW

Name _____ (PLEASE PRINT)

Address _____ Apt.#

City _____ State/Prov. _____ Zip/Postal Code

* Terms and prices subject to change without notice. Sales tax applicable in N.Y.
** Canadian residents will be charged applicable provincial taxes and GST.
   All orders subject to approval. Offer limited to one per household.
   ® are registered trademarks of Harlequin Enterprises Limited.

TEMP99   ©1998 Harlequin Enterprises Limited

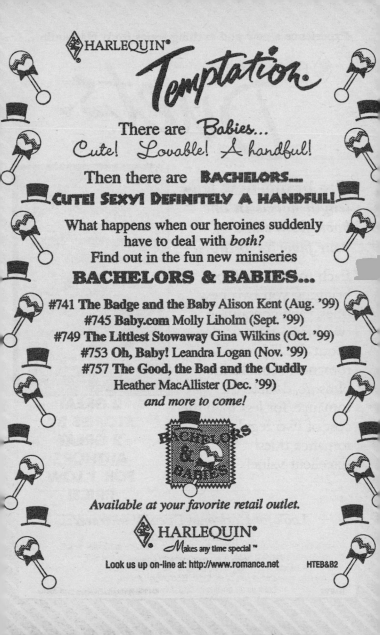

Temptation®

COMING NEXT MONTH

#745 BABY.COM Molly Liholm
Bachelors & Babies

When bachelor Sam Evans finds a baby on his doorstep he's surprised. Little Juliette even comes with a web page and care instructions! *Then* Anne Logan appears on Sam's doorstep. The sexy nanny agrees to help, but soon she doesn't know *who* is more trouble—the teething tot or lovesick Sam!

#746 A CLASS ACT Pamela Burford
15ᵗʰ Anniversary Celebration!

Voted "Most Likely To...Succeed," lawyer Gabe Moreau has done exactly that. But he's never forgotten gorgeous Dena Devlin. Time hasn't erased the hurt...or the hot sizzling attraction between them. Their high school reunion will be the perfect place to reignite those feelings....

#747 NIGHT WHISPERS Leslie Kelly

DJ Kelsey Logan knows what she wants—stuffy but sexy Mitch Wymore. So what if the handsome prof doesn't care for her late-night radio venue "Night Whispers"! It's a show about romance and fantasy—two things Kelsey is absolutely convinced Mitch needs in his life....

#748 THE SEDUCTION OF SYDNEY Jamie Denton
Blaze

Sydney Travers's biological clock is ticking loudly, but there's no suitable daddy in sight. Except Derek Buchanan, who is her best friend and *hardly* lover material. But Sydney has no idea the sexy scientist is in love with her—and determined to seduce Sydney at the first opportunity.